REKINDLED

JEN TALTY

PRAISE FOR JEN TALTY

"If you love stories full of questions and mysteries for you to solve than you will love *Rekindled* by Jen Talty." Long and Short Reviews

"From the first word, Jen Talty grabs you and doesn't let go. On the edge of your seat sizzling romance, she is an author not to be missed. With Rekindled, she pulled me in and held me there, breathless and anticipating the next surprising twist, until the last page was turned."
~KyAnn Waters, multi-published author

Assistant Police Chief Blaine Walker sat in his patrol car in a deserted parking lot on the outskirts of town. The white moon glowed through a thin layer of gray clouds. He was enjoying a bacon cheeseburger from his favorite greasy spoon when dispatch interrupted.

"Could you repeat, please?" Shane asked.

"Gunshots reported at twenty-two-fifty Route Nine. The Mead residence," dispatch said.

"Who reported it?" Blaine asked, tossing his bacon cheeseburger to the passenger seat.

"A neighbor."

"Five minutes from location." Blaine slammed the microphone into the cradle. It was probably backfire from a car speeding down the road. Or perhaps Mr. Mead had resumed target practice.

Blaine flipped a switch, and the police siren screeched once. Red lights flashed across the Minnesota night sky. He peeled the car out into the deserted street. Not much happened in Thief Lake during the day, even less at night, but leave it to his ex-father-in-law to stir things up.

As he pulled into the driveway, an uneasy feeling washed over him. He stepped from his patrol car and adjusted his holster, wishing he'd worn his uniform.

It appeared the Mead mansion had every light on, sending an eerie cast of colors across the lake. A little pale-blue SUV was parked in the driveway with the door open. He walked across the gravel path and placed a hand on the hood. Still warm.

The last few days the temperatures had been on the rise, melting most of the snow, but there was still a chill in the air indicating that Jack Frost hadn't caved to the warmth of spring.

He rested his hand on the butt of his weapon and headed toward the main house just as a bloodcurdling scream echoed from inside. Drawing his weapon, he sidestepped up the stairs and onto the porch. Faint sobs echoed in the stillness of the night.

"Daddy," a woman's voice cried.

Blaine carefully pushed back the main door as he gripped his weapon, finger gently over the trigger. He kept his back against the wood frame as he peered into the foyer. A woman with long, blonde hair knelt on the floor, rocking back and forth, whimpering words he couldn't quite understand. Holding his weapon steady, he stepped into the foyer.

Rutherford Mead's body lay sprawled out on the floor. His arms stretched wide, legs slightly bent to the right. His eyes were open but glossed over. Blood trickled out of his neck onto the wood floor.

Blaine swallowed, but focused his attention on the familiar woman hovering over the body. "Police, ma'am, back away."

The woman gasped and scooted backward. Her hands covered her face, but Blaine knew exactly who sat in front of him. His muscles tensed as he adjusted his aim toward the floor beside her. "What are you doing here?"

"I...I..." She brushed her long, blonde hair from her angelic face. Her hair was longer than

Blaine remembered. She looked up at him with fearful eyes. "Blaine, I..."

His breath hitched at the mere sight of his ex-wife. The blueness of her eyes was still prettier than any summer sky he'd ever seen. The porcelain shine of her skin glittered in the bright light.

"Kaylee," he said, and then cleared his throat. "Put your hands in the air."

She held her arms out to the side, dropping something to the floor. "Call for help," she whispered. "We need to call for help."

He now recognized the object that had fallen from her trembling hands as a portable phone. He reached with his free hand for his cell and called the dispatcher, resting the phone on his ear. With his eyes locked on Kaylee, he bent forward and felt Rutherford's neck for a pulse. "Possible homicide. Get the medical examiner and Chief Whitcomb out here." He snapped his phone shut.

Blaine did his best to control his raging pulse and focus on the situation and not the frightened creature sitting before him. He knew all too well that where Kaylee was concerned, things were never what they appeared to be. It had been years since he'd last seen his ex-wife. Years since anyone, including her father, had seen or heard from her. "What happened here?"

She stared at him for a moment. "I found him like this."

"How long have you been here?" He forced his trembling muscles to hold his aim steady, but not directly on her.

"Five or ten minutes?" Her voice trembled.

"How did you get in the house?"

"The kitchen door."

"Did he know you were coming?" Not that Blaine spoke much to his father-in-law, but last he heard, Rutherford had very little to no contact with his daughter. He'd even cut her from his will shortly after she disappeared. But now rumors had been circulating that he'd changed his will again and left everything to her, making this a very difficult situation.

"You don't think…" Her jaw dropped open as her eyes widened. "Oh God, you do."

"Let's step outside." Blaine holstered his gun and nodded toward the porch.

He laced his fingers around her arm. She twitched, jerking away. Her eyes met his with a combination of fear and confusion. Blackness smudged her pale, stricken face.

"To my car." He took her elbow, just like he would any other suspect or witness. "Sit down, Kaylee." He pulled open the door and helped her in. He stood with his back to her, trying to collect his thoughts. Living in a small town made every case he worked on harder, because he knew everyone on a personal level.

Investigating the death of his ex-wife's father was about as personal as things could get.

Rarely at a loss for words, he let out a breath and focused on the gray, smoke-like puff that formed in the air. The last time he had been unable to utter a single word was the last time he saw her. He pinched the bridge of his nose. "I'm sorry, Kaylee."

He took a blanket out of his trunk and covered her shaking body.

"He left the kitchen door open for me." The blanket curled under her fingers. "Dad never left doors open or lights on unless he knew someone was coming."

"You entered via the kitchen? Then did what?" he questioned, knowing he shouldn't. Their past relationship really put a damper on him being able to control this case.

"I was nervous, so I got a glass of water, and

then I called for him. When I got no answer, I left the kitchen, heading for his office."

"Did you go anywhere else in the house?

"I went from the kitchen to where I found him." Kaylee had curled the blanket up to her chin, her head down.

She was crying, and he wanted to wrap his arms around her and tell her it was all going to be okay.

But it wasn't okay, and not just because her father was dead.

He looked up at the big, white house with the dark-green shutters. With every light on, the house gleamed like a scene straight from *The Exorcist.*

The sound of gravel crunching under large tires caught his attention. His boss's pickup, followed by an ambulance and the medical examiner's car, pulled in. Blaine knelt beside Kaylee, placing his hand on her knee. The moment he touched her, a single spark ignited in his veins, spreading warmth through his body. He yanked his hand away. He had a job to do. Lingering in the past had nothing to do with the present situation, no matter how pretty the past looked.

"I need you to stay right here." A soft scent of strawberries and vanilla filled his nostrils. He leaned across her to grab his keys. The familiar smell reeled in his head like a song you couldn't stop humming. "Where are the keys to your car?"

"In my purse, in the kitchen." Pressure on his bicep stilled him. "Someone killed my father."

"We don't know what happened, but I'll find out." A sudden, sharp pain ripped through Blaine's heart. A murder had occurred on his watch. To make matters worse, he had one possible witness and one possible suspect—his ex-wife. All in all, not a good night.

He nodded to Police Chief Dave Whitcomb as they made their way up to the house. While the door didn't appear damaged, his instincts told him foul play had been involved. However, with her so close, and the gut-wrenching emotions she sparked, his instincts couldn't be trusted.

When he entered the foyer, he stepped around Rutherford's body to see things from a different perspective, while he put on a pair of latex gloves. At first glance, it looked like he might have fallen down the curved staircase. Blood pooled under his head, which could be consistent with a fall, but something didn't feel right.

"Why is it you always have to get me out of bed when you've got the night shift?" Dave rubbed his unshaven face, looking around the foyer. "I won't even mention the uniform issue."

"I never wear it, and you don't have a problem with it." Blaine removed the lens cap from the police-issue camera, flipped on the flash, and photographed the body while Dave made some measurements and scribbled them on a pad. "Besides, have I even seen you in one?"

"Keep taking pictures," Dave said.

"Something's off here." Blaine looked from the staircase to the body. He pointed to the base of the neck, before snapping a picture of an open wound oozing blood.

"That looks like a bullet graze," Dave said, moving to the side, letting the ME in to asses the body.

"I know what it looks like," Blaine muttered. Ten years ago, his life had changed forever when Kaylee had run off to Europe, cutting all ties to Thief Lake, including those to her father. "Someone reported gunshots, which is what brought me here in the first place."

"You see that?" Dave asked the ME.

The ME gently pushed up Rutherford's shirt. "A bullet hole."

Blaine swallowed and then took a few more

pictures. Anyone who might benefit from a death usually looked guilty in the eyes of the public. If Rutherford changed his will, then Kaylee Mead stood to inherit one hefty sum.

"Let's take a look around," Dave said.

"Her purse should be in the kitchen." Blaine followed him down the hall and into the kitchen. Aside from all the lights being on, everything looked normal. "She says she came in through that door, got a drink, and then went looking for him."

"How long?"

"Said five to ten minutes. I heard her scream as I came to the door." The first thing Blaine noted was that indeed her purse was on the kitchen table. He looked inside, gently pushing a few items around until he found her keys. He scanned the room and looked for anything that could take the blame off Kaylee. She was a lot of things, but not a cold-blooded murderer. "Damn."

"What is it?" Dave asked.

"A bullet." Blaine knelt down next to the kitchen table. "Give me a bag." First he took a picture while Dave sketched the dimensions on his pad. Then, using a pocketknife, Blaine dug the bullet out of the table and shoved it in the evidence bag.

"Doesn't look like there was any kind of struggle," Dave commented.

"That's puzzling, isn't it?" Blaine said. "And no blood between the kitchen and foyer."

"Maybe he was having a conversation with someone he thought he could trust, like his daughter?"

Blaine froze and gripped the chair. The overwhelming desire to protect and defend Kaylee bubbled in his bloodstream. Regardless of the rift between father and daughter, and Kaylee's inability to think beyond herself, she couldn't kill someone.

Blaine circled the kitchen table. There had to be a clue. Something that would tell him Kaylee had just stumbled into a bad situation. Anything that could tell him who did this, and why.

No scuff marks on the floor. Nothing out of place. Everything seemed as it should be. Her father believed everything had its place, so Blaine wasn't surprised to see clear and clean countertops. Not a single dish left out. He quickly glanced into the dishwasher. "Kaylee said she had a glass of water. We'll need to dust all these dishes for prints."

"Jonesy and Mac will be here shortly to takeover," Dave commented. "You can't question her."

"I know." Blaine stuffed the camera in the bag as they made their way back to the foyer. "I'll take her to the station and get someone else to take the official statement."

"We have to treat her as a suspect." Dave raised his brow.

"I was first on the scene. Nothing we can do about that. You need to take over here. Call ahead and have someone waiting for us. I won't say five words on the way there." Not talking to her would be a tall order, but it was best. For both of them.

"Don't screw up." Dave shook his head. "So, what do you make of your ex-wife's timely return?"

Blaine cringed. "I'd say it's untimely."

Dave stopped at the front door and turned. "I'm going to search her car." He lowered his chin. "If I find a gun, or anything that gives me cause, I'm going to arrest her."

"I get it." Blaine ran a hand through his shoulder-length hair. No way would he let her out of his sight. If she didn't kill her father, someone else did, and that someone might have seen her.

And since he was probably going to be forced to stay in the background on this one, he'd make sure he'd stay up close and personal with her.

'Untimely' didn't begin to describe his ex-wife's return.

Kaylee's heart pounded against her ribs, reminding her of what a mess her life had turned out to be. Bad luck seemed to follow her wherever she went. Now her father was dead. Murdered. And she was to blame.

She'd come back to town for one reason and one reason only. To get help and money from her father so she'd be able to keep hiding. Keep running. Now she was stuck in a town she'd never wanted to see again and dealing with the man who'd been the reason she'd left in the first place.

Seeing Blaine only made things more difficult. He did things to her insides, rendering her utterly useless. Nothing new there. She silently cursed herself. Blaine shouldn't have any effect on her, not after what he'd done.

She glanced at her childhood home where Blaine was leaning against the wood railing on the front porch, looking exactly the way she remembered him. The same way he haunted her dreams. His straight, black hair still rebel-long, and his skin the color of raw gold. She could smell his faint, musky aftershave lotion as it lingered in the car.

She pulled the blanket up to her chin and shivered, but not from the frigid air. One week ago, she'd collected all her belongings and slipped away into the night. Chicago had been the promise of a new beginning, but once again, she'd made a horrendous mistake.

Blaine tossed a bag over his shoulder and made his way toward the car. He didn't wear a police uniform, but somehow that didn't surprise her.

"I'm sorry that took so long," he said as he ducked his head, seating himself in the driver's seat.

"We were going to try to patch things up and put the past behind us," she tried to explain. But that wasn't the whole truth. Her father had found out about whom she'd been dealing with and knew she was in trouble. Big trouble. He'd offered to help, but only if she returned home. Only if she did things his way. She'd never liked his way much.

"I need you to come to the station and make a statement," Blaine said. "Might be a good idea to call a lawyer."

"I didn't kill my father." She folded her arms across her chest and stared out the window at the side mirror. She watched her father's home disappear into the night. Just like everything else in her life, coming home had been a huge mistake. When she turned to glance at Blaine's strong profile, she noticed the tension in his face matched the white knuckles gripping the steering wheel.

"Save it for the officer doing the questioning. But for the record, we'll be asking you not to leave the area. Also, you can't stay at your father's home until we've had a chance to go through it, top to bottom."

"I really need a lawyer?" The only lawyer she knew these days wanted her out of the picture completely. She rubbed her hands across her jeans and fixed her gaze on the darkness. A thick layer of fog settled across the night like a blanket, but she didn't really need to see anything. Either she was going to jail for something she didn't do or she was going to die for something she did do.

The patrol car rolled to a stop outside the police station. Well, it wasn't much of a station. Just a small building that housed, from what she could remember, the Chief, his assistant, and possibly three or four other officers. This part of the world was still half in the dark ages, but maybe that would turn out to be a blessing. Maybe Nino didn't even know Thief Lake existed. Maybe she was safe.

Blaine stepped from the car and strolled to the other side, opening the door. She took the hand he offered. His warm skin heated her body. "Official statement? Or official interrogation?"

"It's a statement, for now. Just tell us what you know. What happened from the time you pulled into the driveway until I found you." He opened the station door and motioned toward a hallway. "My office is the last door on the left. Wait there for me."

"Sure. A statement." She glanced around the well-lit, tiny lobby. The lights glared, but somehow the place felt dark. "Where are you going?" Fear rippled down her spine. She didn't want to be with him, but she didn't want to be alone. "You're going to arrest me, aren't you?"

He stopped and stared at her for a moment. "I'm going to get us some coffee and snag someone to take your statement since...well, our past. It wouldn't be professional, and I could be accused of clouding the case. Covering something up."

"You have to be kidding me. I found my father..." She sniffled. "You can't think I kill—"

"Kaylee," he said sternly, "We need to know

your side of the story, officially. I'm just doing my job."

"I'd like my coffee black, please." She turned away. 'Officially,' her ex-husband could shove it.

She knotted her fists and rolled them into her lower back as she walked down the hall. Maybe she had a muscle relaxant in her purse.

Crap. Her purse was in her father's house. She stretched her back and rolled her hands again across her aching, burning muscles. She stopped briefly at the edge of the door that had Blaine's name on it before entering.

"Kaylee, I'm so sorry," a male voice echoed in her ears.

"Hadley? What are you doing here?" Hadley Danks, her father's business lawyer, stood in the middle of the white office with his arms stretched wide. She hesitated for a moment. Ever since she'd left Thief Lake, she'd been alone. No one to protect her. No one she could trust. Besides, the last time she'd seen Hadley was the day she found out her father wasn't her father after all.

"How did you know I was here?" The need to feel as though someone out there gave a damn overtook her desire to protect all the walls she had created. She walked into his arms and rested her head on his strong shoulder. Regardless, Hadley had been a source of comfort during her teen years.

"I got a call from Chief Whitcomb saying you might need me."

"Shit," she cursed, stepping back. The whole town was going to think she killed her own father. Not that anyone thought fondly of her anyway. "I found Daddy dead; I didn't kill him." Looking around the office, she realized how bad things were. Under the circumstances, if she were Blaine, she'd think the same thing.

"Let's sit."

The muscles in her back twisted and tightened. Sitting would hurt, so she paced instead. "Who'd want to kill my father?"

"He wasn't the easiest man, Kaylee. He did make an enemy or two over the years."

Blaine entered his office carrying a tray of coffee and doughnuts. "Don't say one word." He eyed them both as he took one of the white powdered jelly ones. "I've heard it all before."

"Must be nice to be able to eat whatever you want and not have an ounce of fat on your body." Kaylee forced her gaze to the floor. She knew firsthand what that body looked like. Six-pack abs, thick biceps, and strong, lean legs. The mere sight of his bronze-colored skin sent a wave of desire through her bloodstream. Her fingertips itched to touch and caress every inch of his supple body. Nope, she didn't want to remember.

The sound of shuffled papers echoed as Blaine sat behind his desk. "Williams, could you come in here, please?" he asked into the speakerphone. "Deputy Williams is going to ask you some questions, record them, and then we'll need you to sign the statement. Do you understand?"

She stared out the window. It had started to rain. She watched the fat raindrops hit the puddles in the parking lot. Nothing in her life had ever gone right. "Don't you have to read me my rights or something?"

"You're not under arrest, but if you choose not to cooperate, you will leave me no choice," Blaine said.

"Kaylee, as the attorney present, I advise you just to answer his questions and tell him what you can remember. If I think there is something you shouldn't answer, I'll let you know," Hadley cut in. "But if this comes down to you really needing a criminal lawyer, I'll get you the best."

Well, that didn't make her feel any better.

"Sit down," Blaine said. "We're going to be here a while."

"Wonderful." She let out a long, slow breath, forcing the muscles in her back to relax as she settled herself in a hard wooden chair across from Blaine's desk. Somehow, she didn't think her life could get any worse.

"Ready, boss," a young man in uniform said. He took a seat with pad and pen in hand.

"Go ahead," Blaine said.

"Did you notice what time you arrived?" Williams asked.

"Around eleven," she replied, trying to tell herself she had nothing to hide but the truth.

"Did you notice anything unusual?" Williams continued.

"Yeah, all the lights were on."

"Why was that unusual?"

"My father hated waste. Leaving unnecessary lights on cost money. He hated wasting money more than anything else."

"Anything else seem out of the ordinary?" Williams looked too serious, only adding to the tension lingering in the air.

"Not really."

"How did you get into the house?" William's asked.

"The kitchen door."

"Why not the front door?"

"Dad never liked leaving the front door unlocked because it's too hard for him to hear anyone entering the house from his office. He said he'd be working late and I should come in through the kitchen." She sat straighter in her chair and glanced toward Blaine. He sat back in his chair, hands folded in his lap, just listening. He'd always been good at his job, she just didn't like being on the other end of it.

"Then what?" Blaine interjected, his tone unemotional and detached.

"I poured myself a glass of water, drank it, and then went to go find him."

"Where did you put the glass?" Williams asked.

She shifted in her seat and glanced toward Hadley. "I put it in the dishwasher."

"Anything else in the dishwasher?"

"Dishes?" She shouldn't expect Blaine, or even this Williams guy, to have any compassion for her, but they were both cold as stone, and that didn't help her growing fear.

"Then what?" Williams's voice echoed.

Her pulse beat so fast it felt like she had just run a marathon. "I called his name a few times. When I didn't get a response, I headed toward his office. You have to go through the main foyer to get to that room."

"Is that when you noticed your father?" Williams asked.

A flash of her father's limp, cold body sprawled out on the floor in a pool of his own blood filled her mind. She nodded, unable to use words.

"I need a verbal response," Williams said.

"Yes."

"What happened next?" Williams questioned.

"I screamed, and then Blaine was there," she replied. Her skin tingled as though she was being pricked by thousands of tiny needles, precisely at the same time.

"What did you touch?" Williams's voice sounded bland, almost like a robot. As if her answers didn't matter because he'd already decided she was guilty.

"Some things in the kitchen. The door. Maybe the table in the hallway. The phone."

"Do you own a gun?"

"No law that says she can't own a gun," Hadley

said. "She's told you what happened. I think we can be done here."

Kaylee glanced toward Blaine. He scowled. "We're not done just yet."

"Miss Mead. Do not leave town," Williams said. "If you do, this department will issue a warrant for your arrest."

"Understand that a crime has been committed and right now you are our only link to solving that crime," Blaine said.

Kaylee opened her mouth, but nothing came out. Not even a gasp. She didn't know what to say, much less what to do. Nino had men everywhere. If an arrest warrant went out, she'd be as good as dead.

"I don't plan on going anywhere."

"That's good to know," Blaine said. He pushed back his chair and clasped his hands behind his head. "Keep going, Williams."

"Miss Mead, would you be willing to give us your fingerprints, hair strands, and let me check your hands for gun powder residue?" Williams said.

"You don't have to give them anything right now," Hadley added, patting her shoulder.

"I'll do it. What else?"

"Nothing until we hear from the ME." Blaine

stood. "Thank you for cooperating." His tone was detached, but when she caught his gaze, a sudden softness filled his eyes. "Williams, why don't you go type up the report and bring it to Kaylee to sign."

"Sure thing, boss." Williams rose.

"Then the real fun begins, huh?" She shifted in her seat, causing a sharp pain to shoot up her spine. She did her best not to wince as she stood. "I didn't kill my father."

"Thanks for coming, Hadley," Blaine said, ignoring her. "I'll be in touch."

Hadley gave her a warm smile and a kind hug. "Don't talk to them. Blaine included. If they want to interview you more, make sure you call me." He handed her his business card. "I know a great criminal lawyer."

The two men shook hands, and Kaylee leaned her hip against the cool window. Steam from rain hitting the cold pavement slowly rose and then dissipated a few inches from the ground. The severity of her life hit her full-force. She fought the tears.

What a mess she'd made of her life. Now she didn't even have the chance to right a wrong with her father. Or find out what her father had wanted to share with her. Another condition of his help.

She had to listen to him no matter how it made her feel. He'd said it was important. "What now?"

"I'm sorry about your father," Blaine whispered.

She hadn't realized he was standing so close to her. His arms wrapped around her shivering body.

She needed the healing powers of human contact, but she couldn't let it be him. "Leave me alone," she snapped.

The tender touch of his thumb across her cheek soothed her. And angered her. "I'm sorry I had to put you through this, but it's my job."

"I resent the hell out of you and your job." She batted his hand away.

"My job can be tricky, but right now," he ran his long fingers through his hair, "I'm just an old friend."

"Yeah, right." Friends didn't betray friends like he had betrayed her so many years ago. "Will you take me to my car so I can go to the motel, *friend*?" Sarcasm had always been her greatest defense and worst enemy, especially where Blaine was concerned.

"We'll get your car in the morning."

"I need my overnight bag," she protested as she followed him out of his office and through the main door toward the parking lot. "I'm not going to run off. Honestly, I have no place to go." Not unless she wanted to end up dead, just like her father.

"I'll take care of everything in the morning." He opened a truck door, waiting for her to get in.

"I can take care of myself. Just take me to my car. And I need my purse." All she wanted was to sink into a hot bath and cry her eyes out. Her body ached. A million thoughts raced through her mind, but she couldn't focus on anything other than her father. She may not have been close to her father, but that didn't mean she didn't love him.

"Get in the truck, Kaylee." Blaine gave her a little push.

"Fine."

The raindrops thumped against the windshield as the wipers sloshed it onto the road. His truck smelled like new leather and cheap perfume, not a good combination. Kaylee glanced out the window. "Hey, this isn't the way to the motel." The town had only one, and they were definitely heading in the wrong direction.

"I know." He slapped the blinker on.

"No way, Blaine Walker. You turn this hunk of steel around and take me to the motel."

"No. You are staying with me tonight," he said, then punched the gas, making the tires squeal.

"Someone may have just murdered your father, and on the night of your return." He pulled his truck in front of his parents' garage. A garage she remembered well.

"If your father was murdered, and I think he was, technically you're a potential suspect." Blaine reached across the truck and put a finger over her lips. "But you could be a target, too. Especially if whoever did this thinks you saw them."

The intensity in his near-black eyes, along with his words, stunned her. She tried to swallow, but her throat was too dry. "I didn't see anyone," she managed. But she knew who was out there, waiting. Maybe staying with a cop wasn't such a bad idea after all.

"They may have seen you."

Panic set in. She wouldn't be able to hide much longer. If at all.

2

"Y ou still live here?" Kaylee asked as she looked to the staircase going up to Blaine's parents' garage apartment. The one they'd lived in together during their short marriage. Puffy, dark clouds floated across the sky, partially covering the half moon. The rain had let up some, but the cold, crisp air chilled her skin.

"I moved back when Dad died. I wanted to be close to Mom, but I didn't want to live with her." He glanced over his shoulder with a scowl, like she should know all this.

"I'm sorry. I didn't know." She wanted to reach out and touch him. He'd always been close to his father. "How? When?"

"Few years ago. Car accident." He turned. "A lot has changed around here."

A loud clicking noise echoed as he unlocked the door at the top of the stairs and pushed it open. The familiar small space did nothing to ease her growing discomfort, and Blaine's physical effect on her only added to her confusion.

She stepped in and glanced around. He wasn't kidding when he said a lot had changed. The apartment she remembered had bare walls, old, blue matted-down carpet and a sagging couch. He'd always been good with his hands, but the new galley-style kitchen she stared at was beyond anything she remembered he could do.

"You do all this work yourself?" She slid her fingers across the log-style chair-rail that set off the soft-blue walls in the main room.

"Gives me something to do when I'm not working. You should see the kitchen in Mom's house. Took me nearly three months."

"I'm sure it's beautiful." A chocolate-colored leather sofa sat in front of a wood-burning fireplace. A bearskin rug hung on the wall. "You have great taste."

He shrugged. "Can I get you some hot

chocolate?" He kicked off his boots and made his way into the kitchen. "I think I've got marshmallows."

"Marshmallows?" As a little girl she had loved to go out and play in the snow, and then when she'd come in all wet and cold, her father would meet her in the kitchen with hot chocolate and marshmallows. The big ones. She'd poke at the white, puffy object floating in a sea of steaming milk chocolate, making sure the marshmallows were totally saturated. That had been the best part.

The realization that her father was actually gone forever sent tears streaming down her cheeks. "Sure," she managed through choking sobs. Her eyes were already puffy from hours of crying over the past few weeks. At twenty-eight, she'd made nothing but one pathetic mistake after another.

"Sit down." Blaine's strong hand pressed gently against her lower back and helped her to the couch.

The soft leather conformed to her body. "Please tell me this is all a bad dream." She clung to his strong frame for support, something she hadn't felt in years. "Please tell me my father didn't die before I had a chance to fix all the wrongs between us," she cried, wrapping her fists in Blaine's T-shirt.

"Let it go," Blaine whispered, stroking his fingers through her hair.

Being in his embrace brought back memories she'd been trying to pretend didn't exist. She'd barely gotten used to the idea of coming home, and to be reminded of what could have been, what had been taken from her, was more than she could handle.

A sense of dread engulfed her as she took a deep breath. "I'm sorry." She pushed herself from his welcoming arms. "I'm just tired." She reminded herself the comfort he was offering wasn't real. Perhaps it had never been real.

He turned sideways on the sofa, his arms no longer around her. "When did you decide to come back to town?"

Dropping her head back on the sofa, she closed her eyes. If he only knew the half of it. "I called him two weeks ago."

"You called him?"

She nodded. She'd give Blaine what little information she could without getting herself into trouble. She knew him well enough to know he'd use whatever information he could pump out of her to get the bad guy. Right now, that could mean her. "We'd been in touch a few times over the last few years. We both wanted to put the past behind us."

He ran his hand across his face, then through his jet-black hair. "I'm stuck between a rock and a hard place here."

"And I shouldn't be talking to you about anything without a lawyer." She looked directly into his stubborn, dark eyes. "Do you honestly believe I could kill my father?"

"Not intentionally."

Anger surged through her blood, but before she could leap from the couch, he grabbed her arm. "Let me go."

"I want to help you."

"By accusing me of something I didn't do?" She yanked her arm free of his grasp and stood, pain rippling down her back. She did her best not show it. "I should've known. You've always held me responsible for what happened."

"Damn it!" His fist smacked the pillow, and he bolted upright. "I'm a cop. It's my job to find out what happened to your father. A job I take very seriously, but that doesn't change the fact that you're still my wife."

"I haven't been your wife for a long time. And you never loved me anyway." A thick lump formed in her throat. Her own father had offered her husband money to divorce her, and her husband had taken the bribe. That was proof enough for her.

"Touché." He turned, uttering a few choice curses as he stormed the five paces to the kitchen, and then ducked his head into the refrigerator. "You don't know what you're talking about."

"I saw the check." She swallowed. "You took my father's money and never looked back."

A swishing noise filled the room when he opened a soda can. She couldn't take her eyes off him while he gulped down his drink. The pain in her chest thumped with every beat of her heart as he took small steps until he stood right in front of her.

"I never took a dime from your father." He narrowed his stare. "And, I might add, you're the one who filed for divorce."

"Can you deny you had the check?" she asked.

"No." He chugged his soda, then slammed it on the coffee table.

"Then you took my father's money." She folded her arms across her middle.

"I ripped it up when he had the audacity to blame me for our son's death."

"Deslin," she spoke his name softly. Her pulse flared, and her hands trembled. No matter how much time had passed, the pain never subsided. Unable to carry her own weight, she sat down. "You blame me for Deslin's death."

"And you blame me." The hardness in his face matched the tone of his voice.

No point in arguing. Nothing had changed. Even if Blaine had never cashed the check, her father had given it to him and he'd contemplated it. And their son was still dead.

A roll of thunder rumbled outside. Lightning flashed in the sky, illuminating the room for one brief second. The rain began to fall so heavily that it sounded like deer running across the roof.

"We both hurt," he whispered. "But you walked away without a word."

For years, she'd dealt with the pain of losing her only son in a silent hell. "This has nothing to do with my father's death." She stretched, letting out a good fake yawn. Dwelling on the past wouldn't help her present situation, and it had nothing to do with her future. If she had one. She needed to get out of this mess and get out of town...fast.

He appeared to study her before standing. "You can take the bed," he offered.

"I'll sleep on the couch." She slapped the cushion. "And only for tonight."

"You can't go to the house until we clear it."

"I'll stay at the motel in town."

"No." He glanced at his watch, dismissing her. "I've got to be at work early."

"But didn't you just work half the night?" She blinked, trying to ignore the soft caress of his hand on her back as he led her toward the stairs.

"I'm on call every second I'm not on duty." He gave her a nudge toward the few steps that lead to the loft-style bedroom and then pulled his hand away.

She followed him up the five short steps into his bedroom. When they had first married, she had complained they didn't have a bedroom and had to sleep in the middle of the family room, so he'd raised the roof and built the loft. She glanced at his strong hands. Back then she thought he could do anything. The memories bombarding her mind confused her.

She took a deep breath, filling her nostrils with a fresh pine scent. "I hate incense." Actually, she missed it. She missed him and that made no sense. She glanced around the loft. An Indian painting hung over the same wood bed that had been their bed, but thankfully he'd gotten a new maroon bedspread.

"It's not incense."

"It's stuff that smells." She shifted her gaze toward the small window overlooking the yard. This was all too familiar and shouldn't make her feel like she'd just come home.

She had no home.

"It helps with my headaches."

"You still get them?" She took the T-shirt he was offering. Those so-called headaches could cripple him. She ran her fingers across his forehead like she'd done a million times before. His skin was still soft, but this time he furrowed his brow and took a step back.

"I've actually gone to see a real doctor about them. He put me on some beta blocker thing."

"Is it working?"

"I'll take the fifth." He gave her a slight smile before his face turned serious as he cupped her chin. "I have a job to do. You might not like some things I say, but know one thing." He tightened his grip. "I don't believe you could kill anything, much less your father."

The following morning, Blaine stepped out onto the small porch overlooking the backyard. Spring was still struggling to break through the dense chill of winter. A crisp breeze ruffled his hair across his face. Setting the coffee mug aside, he dug into his jeans pocket and took out a ponytail holder.

The cold air felt good against his bare chest as he pulled his hair through the elastic. He tilted his head toward the wind and took a deep breath of the great outdoors.

"You're going to catch a cold, young man," his mother's voice called from below.

"Old wives' tale." He turned. His mother stood on the back patio of the main house. Five years ago, he'd moved back after his father died in a freak car crash. It had been a temporary situation, until he could find a job, since he'd been put on suspension from the last one. When Dave offered him the Assistant Chief's position, he really didn't have a choice. No one else would hire him.

"Well, you're going to give Mrs. Jennskin a heart attack. Not sure if she's seen a half-naked man in years."

"She sees me every morning." He blew into his coffee and then took a sip. "I do this just for her benefit."

"You're too conceited for your own good." She tugged at her robe. "Now get a shirt on, and I'll make you some breakfast."

"Anything interesting in the morning news?"

His mother nodded and then waved him down.

He'd bet his next month's paycheck that in a million years, his mother wouldn't think he'd bring Kaylee home. Boy, was his mother in for the shock of a lifetime.

After he put his T-shirt on, he taped a note to the refrigerator telling Kaylee to call him as soon as she got up, and then he headed down to join his mother.

"Did you see her?" his mom asked as he stepped into the kitchen.

"I did." Not much had changed between him and Kaylee. They still blamed each other for things beyond their control, and sparks still flew like it was Independence Day. "Can I eat first?" He sat down at the table where a large plate of bacon and eggs waited for him. "Thanks, Mom."

"Yeah, well, thank me by telling me what on God's green earth happened. And how is poor Kaylee?"

"The ME's report isn't back yet, but I think it's safe to say Rutherford was murdered." He shoved some eggs into his mouth, not really tasting the food. The rumor mill in a small town would twist this thing right into a tornado, hurling Kaylee at every turn.

"That poor child. She's been through so much."

"She thinks I took Rutherford's money," he said, glancing toward his mother.

She shook her head. "And she thinks you ran off."

"Excuse me?" He set his fork down. "Why would she think that?"

"Isn't that what you did?" She lowered her chin, giving him her best evil eye.

"Mom, what are you keeping from me?"

"I called you, and called you, and tried to talk to you about Kaylee, but you always hung up on me."

"Because you didn't get it. She left me. Never even said goodbye. Just up and left."

"I'll give you that." Shima sat down next to him and touched his hand. "But she came back."

"Come again?" He arched a brow.

"A few days after you left, she returned. I tried to tell you, but you wouldn't listen."

Blaine blinked. He wondered if maybe he'd taken up sleepwalking or something, because he couldn't believe his ears. "Why didn't you tell me?"

"You're such a stubborn fool. I told you to come home and deal with her before making any rash decisions, but you didn't listen."

Blaine stuffed his mouth again and tried to swallow his damn pride along with his food. He remembered that conversation and a thousand more like it. He ended up giving his own mother the cold shoulder, not answering her phone calls for about a month. The last time they'd talked about Kaylee, he'd told his mother if she wanted him to stay in touch, she'd never bring up Kaylee's name again. His mother had kept her end of the bargain.

"What about Dad? Why didn't he tell me?"

"You know he adored Kaylee." His mother stood and gathered the plates.

"But he hated Rutherford," Blaine muttered.

"Your father never hated anyone, but he knew how Rutherford operated and worried about you going off half-cocked."

"Rutherford didn't think I was good enough for Kaylee." Blaine stood and helped his mother with the dishes. He doubted his heritage had anything to do with why Rutherford disliked him so much. Rutherford Mead didn't like many people, and treated those who worked for him like they were the armpits of the earth.

"She was his little girl, and you were—"

"The Native American bad boy corrupting her."

"That's not true," his mother scolded. "No one would have been good enough for that man."

"Especially the son of the man he'd hired only to fill his quota of minorities."

She tugged at his ponytail. "I'm going to pretend you didn't say that. Now, I have to get ready for my day with bright, young, walking puddles of hormones."

"Can I take the extra eggs and bacon to Kaylee?"

His mother whipped her head around. "She's here?"

"She couldn't go back into the house; it's a crime scene. And I couldn't let her stay in a motel all by herself."

"I least I know I raised a gentleman."

He nodded. "I'll just take this up to her, and then I've got to get to work."

"Tell her where the key to the house is, and she can make herself at home."

"I doubt she will, but thanks." Taking his mother by the hand, he bent over and kissed her forehead. "It's supposed to be my day off, but this murder might have me working day and night."

Blaine stepped out of his mother's home and glanced toward the garage apartment. He still had a lot to learn about where and why Kaylee took off all those years ago, but how was he supposed to know she'd come back? She'd never tried to contact him until she filed for divorce. She'd never loved him. They'd married only because she'd been pregnant. Something he should've accepted ten years ago. Something he planned on doing right now.

———————

Kaylee had tossed and turned most of the night and only partly because of the pain in her back. Every time she'd closed her eyes, she'd seen her father, lifeless on the foyer floor.

She heard a noise downstairs, and the smell of bacon filled the room. She sat up and tugged the handmade afghan aside. Blaine hated to cook, but he loved bacon. She padded to the railing that looked over the family room.

"Glad you're awake," he called. "My mom made breakfast."

"Your mother knows I'm here?" She swallowed. The last conversation she'd had with his mother hadn't gone too well. Shima had given her a piece of her mind about running off, and then told her if she really loved Blaine, she'd give him some peace. Kaylee took that as, 'get the hell out of my son's life.'

Kaylee climbed down the short flight of stairs to the family room. "Thanks, that smells great." She brushed her hair behind her shoulders.

"And here's the hot chocolate you didn't get last night. With marshmallows." He handed her a mug of cocoa with two large marshmallows floating in the steaming liquid.

"Hmmm." The steam floated up, warming her face. She stuck her finger in the cup, dunking the marshmallow. "My favorite."

"I remember," he said softly.

"May I ask you a question?"

He leaned his hip against the kitchen counter. His eyes appeared softer than they had last night. "Sure."

"When did my father give you that check?"

"He never gave it to me. It just appeared in my coat pocket the day of the funeral." He continued to stare at her with unnerving calm.

She dropped her gaze to the mug. She wasn't sure if she wanted to know his version of the truth. "When did you find it?"

He leaned a little closer and whispered in her ear, "After you left." His tone was cruel and unforgiving. "My turn."

"For what?"

"For some answers."

He took the mug and set it aside, pinning her against the counter by his long, ripped body. He didn't touch her, but his arms were on either side of her and his glorious mouth just inches from hers. She took a long, slow breath.

"Why didn't you try to find me when you came back?" he asked.

"So, your mother did tell you," she said.

"I just found out this morning you had come back. Why didn't you try to find me?"

"Isn't it obvious?"

"Nope," he said.

She searched his face for any hint of what he might be thinking or feeling, but she only got a contradiction. His eyes conveyed something sensitive, but his stiff expression and rigid body indicated anger. "You left. You swore you'd never leave this place, but you did. I think that said it all."

He pushed back and crossed his arms across his broad chest. "I guess so, since you filed for divorce shortly after."

"You made it very clear how you felt when you quit your job and left town," she said.

"I just responded to you leaving first."

She let out an exasperated sigh. "Can we just agree we left each other and leave it at that?"

He had the nerve to shrug. Like their marriage had meant less than the paper it had been written on. "Sure."

She reached for the mug, but her muscles cramped. She tried to fight the pain, but the cramping tightened more. Without the muscle relaxants, she was at the mercy of constant pain. She crumpled forward, and hot chocolate splattered out on her hands as pain shot up her spine like a knife ripping through her skin.

"What the...?" He was at her side in seconds, lifting the mug from her shaking hand. "What's wrong?"

"It's just a stiff back." She knotted her fist and started rubbing her lower back, easing the muscle cramps.

"Let me."

"No." She pulled away when he tried to lift her shirt.

"You're obviously in pain. Let me help." Warm pressure from his fingers glided across one of her scars.

"I don't want your help," she snapped.

"Holy shit, Kaylee," he muttered, lifting up her shirt. "What the hell happened?"

His fingers traced a gentle path across each of her scars. Tears stung her cheeks as she pulled the fabric back down and turned. She met his questioning gaze. "Please, not now."

"Those look like…"

"I know what they look like, and I don't want to talk about it." She forced her body upright. "I need to get out of here."

"Until I know exactly what happened to your father, you're not going anywhere." He snagged his keys off the counter.

"You can't make me stay here."

"Yes, I can." He glared at her. "Don't leave this house. I'll get all your things sent over within the hour," he said. "Don't make me arrest you." He slammed the door, knocking the picture of some Indian Drum off the wall.

"You wouldn't dare," she whispered, but deep down she knew he'd do it. Arching her back, she could still feel the cold metal stab into her muscles over and over again. Was it possible that the same man who had been hired to kill her just a few short months ago had successfully killed her father? If that were the case, Kaylee's ex-fiancé would be back soon to finish the job.

3

Kaylee stood in the middle of Blaine's family room and had no idea what to do. He'd brought her car back, along with all her things, but then took her car to the station. He didn't trust her, but hell, she was going to run. She had no choice.

She rummaged through her bag and grabbed her muscle relaxants. If she didn't get back on her regular routine, God only knew what would happen. In the hospital, she'd been afraid she would never walk again. Now she wondered if she'd ever go a day without pain.

She padded to the kitchen, got herself a glass of water, and glanced around. While the apartment felt homey, it didn't really look lived in. It was decorated with nice paintings and furniture, but nothing personal. No pictures of family or friends lined the walls or mantel.

She snagged her cell and stared at it. She'd gotten one of those prepaid cell phones to help her feel safe. Like she could call someone if she needed to. But she half expected Nino to be texting and calling the new number. But there was no text. No unmissed phone call. Nino didn't just give up. She wondered how long she had and what she should tell Blaine. As an officer of the law, he'd have to protect her, but what would he do with her when he discovered what she'd done?

And then there were her emotional and physical reactions to Blaine. They were basically strangers to each other, yet there seemed to be some cosmic connection that hadn't dissolved. She'd have to be dead not to notice the fire still burning behind his touch.

She marched up the stairs and started searching his room for something that said he lived here or that he had a life. No pictures of girlfriends, or even his father, were on his nightstand. Not a single magazine or book to be found.

She opened up a couple of drawers and

laughed. At least that hadn't changed. He was still a stuffer. She pulled out a pair of wrinkled sweats. She fanned them and decided they looked and felt a whole lot more comfortable than wearing the same clothes from last night.

Slipping her legs into the soft fabric, she tried not to laugh at herself. She'd done this same thing when Blaine had been working nights when they were first married. She'd get lonely and thought being in his clothes would help.

She gave up on finding anything personal. Maybe he'd always been like this. When she'd moved in, she had been the one who brought all the pictures. Back in the day, she'd been a sentimental sap. But today, she didn't have that luxury.

She plopped herself down on the sofa in Blaine's sweatpants and one of her camisoles. The soft, fuzzy blanket tickled her skin as she wrapped it around her body. She found the remote for the television and started flipping through the channels in hopes of ridding her thoughts of Blaine, so she could focus on an exit strategy.

But all that happened was that her body craved sleep, so she let her eyelids drop, and she relaxed into the soft cushions. The television barely registered in her ears when a familiar voice snapped her out of a light doze. Stretching, she forced her eyes to flutter open.

"Kaylee? Are you in here?" Shima's voice filled the small space.

Kaylee cleared her throat. "Yep," she managed as she pulled the covers to her chin and sat up. "Right here." She waved and then rubbed the sleepiness from her eyes.

"I'm sorry. I didn't mean to wake you." Shima set down a mug of steaming milk chocolate. "I'll just come back later."

"It's all right." Kaylee curled her legs up, tucking her feet under her bottom. Taking the mug, she sniffed the hot chocolate. "Thank you."

"Did you have lunch? I could make you something to eat."

"No, but thanks." Kaylee took another sip of the cocoa. An uncomfortable silence filled the room, and Kaylee fiddled with her nails. "I...I won't be staying long. Just until I can bury my father and—"

"You're welcome here anytime and for as long as you need." Shima shifted on the couch, moving closer. "I'm sorry about Rutherford."

"Thanks," Kaylee managed.

"Blaine's just doing his job," Shima commented as if she could read Kaylee's thoughts.

"I suppose." Kaylee dropped her head back, closing her eyes. She wasn't sure what was worse. Being chased by the mob. Or being a suspect in her father's murder. Both had their downside.

"I don't mean to imply you'll need one, but have you spoken with a criminal lawyer?"

"Hadley said he'd find me one if it came to that," Kaylee said. "But I didn't do anything wrong." At least not where her father's death was concerned.

Shima patted Kaylee's thigh. "I don't think you killed your father, dear, but I know how the system works. You found him; therefore, you are suspect number one."

"Great," Kaylee muttered. Life certainly didn't like her much these days. Maybe it had never liked her. "Hadley will handle it."

"I have a friend who's a criminal lawyer; I'd like you to talk to her." She handed Kaylee a business card.

Kaylee placed the card next to her mug. Blaine's parents had always been good to her. Welcomed her when her father wanted to disown her. Treated her like family "Shima?"

"Yes, dear?"

"Has Blaine told you something I should know?"

Shima shook her head. "He only told me that you were here. We both want to help you though this."

"Thanks," Kaylee said. The softness in Shima's expression couldn't be ignored.

Shima reached out and ran the backs of her fingers across Kaylee's cheek. "I know I might have said some things to you long ago that I shouldn't have, but I was worried that the two of you had gotten yourselves in over your heads."

"That we did." Kaylee took a deep breath. "We were just kids ourselves. We had no business getting married or having a baby."

"But you did, and too many people tried to interfere, myself included. I'm sorry."

"So am I." Kaylee picked up her cocoa and took a long sip. Shima had always made it with real milk, and it was still the best in town. "I'm going crazy not knowing what happened. I don't even know if I should be planning his funeral, or what."

"I'm sure Hadley will know what to do." Shima rose. "I'll let you rest. Tell Blaine I've got a meeting around seven, and if I don't see him tonight, I'll see him in the morning. And Kaylee?" Shima stopped at the door. "Let Blaine help you. He knows what he's doing."

Kaylee leaned against the doorjamb as Shima glided down the staircase toward the house. The sun had begun its descent behind the horizon and a red glow gleamed across the sky. The air was still but cold. Kaylee wrapped her arms around her middle.

If Nino De Luca had any idea where she'd gone, then he was already here. He wouldn't think twice about teaching her what happened to those who ran out on a De Luca. Being arrested for her father's murder and going to jail seemed safer than hanging out over Blaine's garage, waiting for someone to come stick a knife in her back. Again.

———

Blaine tossed the ME's report across his desk. It didn't tell him anything he didn't already suspect. Rutherford's death was ruled a homicide. Some of the injuries could be consistent with a fall down the stairs, except for the bullet in his stomach.

"I didn't think you'd like that report," Dave said, standing in the doorway.

"Just makes our job that much more difficult."
Blaine leaned back in his chair.

"This one is my job and my job alone."

"You can't completely take me off the case. You and I, and Williams, are the only full-timers here." But Blaine certainly understood Dave's position.

"You can do grunt work. Analyze shit, but everything comes by me. You can't do anything officially without me okaying it." Dave raised a brow.

"Fine," Blaine said. "Did Jonesy and Mac find anything?"

"Other than Kaylee's gun?" Dave shook his head. "It was registered as Kaylee Walker."

Blaine's heart jolted for a brief moment as he filed those words into the scheme of things. She kept his name? "Does it match the bullet found at the scene?"

"Nine millimeter, but Rutherford owned two, and your personal weapon is the same."

"Half the town probably owns a nine millimeter."

Dave leaned over the desk and hit the intercom button. "Stacey, get someone to go to Blaine's house and pick up Ms. Mead for some more questioning."

"Sure thing," Stacey replied.

"I'd better warn her," Blaine said as he picked up the phone and dialed his home number.

"Did Williams fingerprint her? Swab her hands?"

Blaine closed his eyes for a brief moment, allowing the flash of anger to lessen before he spoke. "Everything was done by the book."

"She stayed at your house last night, and the book has nothing to do with that."

"I couldn't let my ex-wife stay at a motel alone."

"When was the last time you fired your personal weapon?" Dave gave him an apologetic glance.

"Three days ago," he said, lifting the phone to his ear. "I'll take the residue test, and any other test you want, right after I get—" A click rang in his ear indicating someone had answered.

"Walker Residence." Kaylee's voice sang in his ears, turning the boiling rage rushing through his veins into something he didn't want to acknowledge.

"Hey." His voice caught, and he had to clear his throat. "I've sent someone to bring you down to the station."

"Wh…why?"

Pinching the bridge of his nose, the nausea rose up from his gut. It had been three months since his last migraine, and today wouldn't be a good day to get one. "Your father's death was ruled a homicide," he said as compassionately as he could. "I'll call Hadley."

"No," Kaylee said with conviction in her voice.

"Kaylee, it's for your own protection. We might have to—"

Dave waved his hand. "Her gun hadn't been fired," he whispered.

That didn't make Blaine feel better.

"I understand that, but he's not a criminal lawyer. I'm not sure he's ever seen the inside of a courtroom."

"You need a good lawyer, and Hadley is just that."

"Shima recommended someone else. Her name is—"

"Emma Peterson." Good Lord in heaven. What the hell was his mother thinking?

"You know her?"

"I'll call her for you." Blaine rubbed his neck. "Someone should be there any minute."

"I'll be ready."

"You can't question her. I'll send Williams in."

"I'm going to have to be able to ask something.

You can't tie my hands so tightly that it will weaken the department."

"Williams does the questioning." Dave stepped out of Blaine's office. The timing couldn't have been more perfect for the man to leave.

Spots flickered about in front of Blaine's eyes. He reached for his desk drawer, pulling out a shot of his medication, and prayed like hell it would work. He winced as he jabbed himself with the needle.

He smacked the intercom button. "Stacey, call Emma Peterson and tell her I need her in my office ASAP. Tell her it's about the Rutherford Mead murder. And tell Williams to be in my office in ten minutes." He pushed his chair back, dropped his head between his knees, and breathed deeply.

He forced himself to inhale through his nose and breathe out of his mouth. The nausea had eased up, but the pounding between his ears had only intensified. He stayed like that for a long moment—at least five minutes—letting the medicine take over. His pulse slowed and his body relaxed, but he knew this migraine wasn't going away.

"Blaine?" Stacey said, stepping into his office with a mug in her hands. "Miss Peterson said she'd be here in about fifteen minutes." Stacey set the cup of coffee on his desk. "Caffeine is supposed to help."

He looked up at his secretary. "I'm fine, but thanks."

"Also, Jonesy is pulling in with Kaylee."

"Bring her down." He took the coffee and sipped. He ran a hand across his damp forehead. "Ask Dave to join us," he yelled, holding his throbbing head. Kaylee was wreaking havoc on his system. He looked out the window, collecting himself.

"I know that look." Kaylee seemed to appear out of nowhere and stood a few feet from him, looking just like the young girl he had fallen in love with so many years ago. "Migraine?" Her long, blonde hair flowed over her shoulders, and she had that soft smile on her angelic face that she'd always greeted him with.

That did nothing to help the pain bouncing between his ears. He nodded, unable to say anything.

"Why am I here?" she asked, stepping around his desk. Clasping her hands together, she rubbed them vigorously before she raised them to his forehead, applying the perfect amount of pressure.

Her soothing fingers eased his pain, and not just in his head. "No one has hands like you." He relaxed in his chair.

"Did you call that lawyer? What was her name? Patterson or something?"

"Emma Peterson." He stood, pulling himself from her touch. "I had my secretary call her. She should be here shortly." Just his luck. His ex-wife and his ex-girlfriend in the same room. When he and Emma had dated, she'd accused him of still being in love with Kaylee. He'd denied it, of course, but he also knew there was a ring of truth to her words. He walked to the window and stared at the few clouds floating about the blue sky. He hadn't loved Emma, but that didn't matter in the end.

"Your mother said Ms. Peterson is a friend of hers."

"I wouldn't go that far."

Blaine's cell phone vibrated on his hip. "Walker."

"What is this about Rutherford Mead?" Emma bellowed. "Isn't that your ex-wife's father?"

"Yes, and she needs your help." He glanced to Kaylee, who was sitting down with a frown on her beautiful face.

"Oh, just great. You're an asshole, you know that?"

"If it makes you feel better, you're the last person I would've suggested. My mother recommended you to her."

"Your mother? Well, I suppose that shouldn't surprise me."

Blaine didn't want to hate Emma, but part of him would never be able to forgive her. She'd been right about one thing, though. He'd been unable to get over Kaylee. Not something he liked to admit. "She's in my office."

"I'm five minutes out."

Blaine closed his phone. He wanted to continue to stare out the window, because he knew facing Kaylee at the moment wouldn't be a pleasant experience, but he turned anyway.

"If you wouldn't have called her, why is she coming?" Kaylee shifted in her chair, her pale face drained of color.

"Because you said you wanted her."

"I'm not in the mood for games," Kaylee snapped. "I'm your only suspect in a murder I didn't commit and now you're setting me up with a lawyer you wouldn't call. There are so many conflicts of interest here, it's insane."

"She's a good lawyer, one of the best. I wouldn't have called her for different reasons." He filled his lungs with air, but got a jolt of strawberries and vanilla instead. "She doesn't have to like you to help you."

"What have you gotten me into?" she asked.

The reflection of the sun hitting her soft-blue eyes showed all her vulnerabilities. It was hard not to feel for the woman. "I'm trying to keep you out of trouble."

Her lips parted as if she was going to say something, but she stared at him instead.

"Please trust me," he whispered as he took a tentative step toward her. He could no longer resist the primal need to touch her. When he pulled her to his chest, she felt perfect. The desire to feel the connection he'd had with her was stronger than the desire to protect his own heart.

Her fists pushed against his chest. "I don't trust you."

"Excuse me," Emma said, then cleared her throat. "I need to talk to my client." She gave Blaine a deadly glare. "Alone."

The pounding in his head erupted once again. "You've got to trust me," he said.

Wide, frightened eyes blinked at him. "You don't make it easy."

"You've got ten minutes." Without giving either woman a second glance, Blaine left the office.

"Gee, thanks," Emma said.

Kaylee eyed the professional woman pulling out all sorts of papers from her briefcase, trying to figure out the real connection between Emma and Blaine.

Kaylee knotted her fists and applied pressure to the base of her back before she settled down into one of the most uncomfortable chairs in the world.

"Do you know why the police have asked you to the station?"

Well, Emma didn't hold back any punches. "I'm the one who found my father. All Blaine said was that they were treating this as a homicide." While Emma flipped open a legal pad, Kaylee noticed how rigid Emma appeared. She wore her dark-brown hair in a tight ponytail. Her face was expressionless. She sat like she had a stick shoved halfway up her ass. Emma just looked cold.

"You found your father dead," Emma said.

"Yes," Kaylee said.

"What happened next?"

"Blaine showed up."

Emma arched a brow. "You didn't call for help?" Emma studied her with suspicious eyes.

"I was about to, but Blaine got there first. I had the phone in my hand." Kaylee's pulse tripled.

"Do you know how he died?"

"Blaine said he'd been shot."

"Do you own a gun?"

"Yes." Kaylee tried not to show her fear.

Emma jotted something down, then asked, "Did you kill your father?"

Kaylee shifted her gaze, narrowing at Emma's unnerving eyes. "No."

"Okay. Let's get Blaine back in here and get on with this."

"Wait." Kaylee shifted to get a better look at Emma. "I'd like to ask you a few questions." She felt a coldness glide across the air like morning frost.

"Ask away," Emma said, not moving a muscle, staring directly at Kaylee. It was a bit unnerving.

"Shima recommended you, but I get the feeling you—"

"My personal life doesn't affect my professional one."

At this moment Kaylee wondered if she was

dealing with the ice princess herself. "Hadley Danks—"

"Is not a criminal lawyer. However, I will be consulting him since he's handling your father's estate. He should be here…" she glanced at her watch, "in about a half hour to go over some things with us." Emma brought her icy glare back to Kaylee.

"That's another issue," Kaylee said.

"What?"

"I don't have much money, and I wouldn't be surprised if my father left me nothing. I'm not sure how I could pay you."

Emma showed the first spark of emotion, a slight flicker of amusement in her eyes, and Kaylee's confidence faltered, but she hoped she didn't show it. "We'll worry about that if Blaine arrests you." She paused and ran her fingers through her ponytail. When she looked back at Kaylee, a softness had cut through her frigid exterior and she looked close to human. "Let's hope it doesn't come to that. The fact that he called me before an arrest tells me he's only trying to protect you."

"I didn't kill my father."

"I believe you." Emma rose and held her hand

out. "It's important that you cooperate with the police, but there are certain things I will recommend that you don't do. Trust me. This is what I do for a living."

"It's hard to trust a woman I just met."

"I understand," Emma said. "But I know you, your family history, and I believe you didn't kill your father." She turned to the door and called for Blaine.

4

"Why do we have to wait for Hadley?" Kaylee asked after Blaine announced the latest round of questioning wouldn't begin for a while. "I want to get out of here." She'd been in Blaine's mundane office for over an hour now, and nothing about the off-white, blank walls appealed to her.

His desk was cluttered with files. She glanced up at the water stains lining the drop ceiling. She'd only seen the inside of police a station on television or in the movies, and they didn't look like this. Even the white blinds looked like a blue light special that wasn't such a good deal after all.

The tiny office was already cramped with her, Blaine, the ice princess, and Dave.

"Unless you're going to charge my client, I suggest you get on with this," Emma said with her legs crossed at her ankles. "We're going above and beyond what one would consider *cooperation*. Kaylee doesn't have to be here." Emma reminded Kaylee of a nasty blizzard that the world wanted to hide from in the warmth of their homes, but enjoyed watching from their windows.

"Hadley's bringing Rutherford's will, and I'd like you to hear it," Dave said.

"Why?" Emma asked.

"Because it doesn't help your client," Hadley said as he strolled into Blaine's office. "And this isn't the right way to go about these things. The reading of the will shouldn't be done in the coldness of your office." He waved his finger in the direction of Blaine. "Jesus, the man was your father-in-law."

Emma dropped her pen.

"Someone needs to tell me exactly what the hell is going on," Kaylee said. Fear rippled down her spine, but she'd learned over the last few years to absorb that fear inward. Her father had sent her his will five years ago, and she wasn't in it. If he had changed it since then, her status as possible suspect would probably jump to murderer in less than the time it took to say murderer.

"Don't speak unless I tell you it's okay," Emma said. "And considering Blaine is your ex-husband... I will say for the second time, I don't like him present."

"I'm his boss," Dave said. "This is my investigation. He stays."

"Then he needs to stop interrogating my client."

Blaine removed the ponytail holder and raked his hand through his long, dark hair, then dropped the hair tie back in his desk drawer. When his headaches got too much, he couldn't even pull back his hair because it hurt too much. "For the record, Miss. Peterson, this is an interview. Different from an interrogation."

Kaylee wanted to scream. "I'm fine with him here. Could we just get on with it?"

Hadley set his briefcase down and pulled out some papers. "As of two months ago, Rutherford Mead changed his will, leaving his entire estate to his daughter— lock, stock, and barrel." Hadley glanced around the room. "No one else is named in the will."

"That doesn't mean my client did anything—"

Blaine cut Emma off. "No one's accused her of

anything." He rubbed his temples. "She gets it all? Investments. The business. Everything?"

"The business is a separate entity, but she gets his proceeds unless she wants to sell his portion. But as far as everything else, she gets it all except for one special instruction."

Kaylee could only imagine what his special instruction would be. Knowing her father, it would be something so personally offensive to Kaylee that she wouldn't want his money. "What's the condition?"

"If Kaylee chooses not to take ownership of the estate, she can't sell it. Ownership reverts to—"

"The Church of the Risen Christ," Kaylee said.

"Actually, ownership will go to Blaine Walker," Hadley said.

"Blaine? What the hell?" Kaylee said. Her father had never approved of Blaine or his family. Even though Blaine's father had been one of the top executives in his money management firm, he didn't like the man much. Trusted him even less.

"Yeah, why me?" Blaine asked dryly.

"I guess now that Rutherford is dead, I can say this."

"Say what?" Kaylee asked, her mind spinning. Nothing made sense. Her father wouldn't just give

Blaine anything, unless it meant getting him out of her life.

"Rutherford told me that he never wanted to lay eyes on Reverend Jack Hicks or his wife again. And he needed to make right a lot of wrongs."

"That doesn't make sense. Jack was one of Rutherford's best friends," Blaine said. "This was how long ago?"

"A few weeks ago," Rutherford said. "He signed the final documents in my office less than a month ago."

Kaylee tried to clear her mind and think this through. Her father could be a ruthless man, but he wasn't vindictive. That church meant something to him, so for him to do that, he would have had to have a very good reason. "Do you have any idea why? Because it sounds like some weird twisted form of revenge on either myself or Blaine or both."

"It wasn't that," Hadley said. "But he wouldn't fill me in on the details."

Kaylee had known from the moment she had decided to come back to Thief Lake that she'd have to tell someone her troubles. She just thought that someone would have been her father. Not his attorney, her ex-husband, or her husband's lover, if her suspicions were right about Emma and Blaine

"Two months ago—"

"Ms. Mead—" Emma started, but Kaylee hushed her by putting up a hand. Sitting in jail might actually be safer.

"I called my father seeking money and help after recovering from a serious injury." Kaylee rose, ignoring the stares from the people around the room and went to the window. She wished for rain, but only so she could watch it drip from the sky so while she told her story, she didn't have to actually relive it.

"What kind of injury?" Blaine asked. His voice was riddled with concern and anger.

"I was attacked in my apartment six months ago." Kaylee's muscles constricted as if she were being stabbed all over again. "During my recovery, I realized I was in deep trouble and asked my father for help. After a few arguments, he agreed, and here I am."

"What kind of trouble?" Blaine asked.

"Don't answer that," Emma said.

"I'll ask the questions," Dave said. "What kind of trouble, Ms. Mead?"

She swallowed and turned from Blaine's

burning eyes. "Mostly financial, and some personal issues with my ex-boss."

"When did you leave to come here?" Dave continued.

"A little over a week ago."

"It took you a week to get here from Chicago?" Blaine asked.

"I'll do the questioning," Dave said again. "Why did it take you a week?"

"I had to stop because of back pain and other problems that came from the attack." Not to mention making sure she wasn't being followed and driving in a few circles.

"Do you have receipts? Credit card information about where you stayed during that week?" Dave questioned.

Kaylee could feel Blaine staring at her. She remembered his tender touch this morning when he'd ran his fingers over her scars.

"I paid for everything with cash."

A single, dark cloud crossed the sun's path, dimming the office. She knew deep down this situation was only going to get worse.

"Can you give me names of the towns you stayed in? The hotels?" Dave continued the questioning.

"Can I speak to Blaine alone?" Kaylee turned and looked at him. "Please."

"Not without your lawyer present, you don't. Why don't you talk to me first?" Emma stood, placing a firm hand on Kaylee's forearm.

"Her prints match those on the kitchen door, the sink, the dishwasher, and the table next to the stairs," Dave said, leaning against the doorjamb. "Which is everything she told us she touched. Her gun didn't test positive, and her hands were clean. No gun residue."

"I've never fired it," Kaylee said.

"Not even when you bought it?" Hadley asked.

"Don't answer that," Emma said.

"She wouldn't have to; she's a damn good shot." Blaine let out a dry chuckle.

Kaylee bit back a smile when she locked gazes with Blaine. When they had started dating, he decided to teach her how to shoot. She pretended to play dumb, and then proceeded to shoot three cans sitting way too close to his Mustang. He hadn't known her father had taken her duck hunting all the time.

"Even though her prints were in the house, she found her father, and the issue with the will, we have no reason to believe she killed her father. On the other hand, she's a person of interest."

"That's one way to make a suspect feel at home and say things that could be misconstrued and twisted a half-dozen ways," Emma said.

"You know that's not how we work," Dave said.

Kaylee was getting tired of everyone arguing. "I will answer any and all questions."

"I need a word with you." Dave motioned to Blaine.

"Excuse me." Blaine glided across the office and out into the hallway with Dave.

"Okay, Ms. Mead, start talking." The ice princess pulled out a legal pad, forcing Kaylee back to reality. "What are you hiding?"

"Why do you think she's hiding anything?" Hadley asked.

Emma continued to stare into Kaylee's eyes. The woman's resolve was maddening. Not to mention she no longer felt like the ice princess. "Because she only said she was attacked. Didn't say by who. If it was random. No details. You're hiding something, what is it?"

"Nothing."

"Who attacked you?" Emma said. "Are they in jail? Could they have killed your father?"

"This has nothing to do with my father's death," Kaylee said, but she couldn't be sure, and she wasn't ready to tell anyone anything. "Trust me on that."

"Your father did tell me you were in trouble," Hadley said.

"My medical bills were piling up, and I had a shit job."

"What was your job?" Emma asked.

"I was an executive secretary in a law firm."

"Really? Not necessarily a shit job." Emma actually cracked a smile. "What kind of law firm?"

"Mostly business stuff."

"In the city?" Emma jotted things down on her legal pad.

"Are you my lawyer or a cop?"

Emma let out a long breath, closed her hands in her lap, and very slowly tilted her head toward Kaylee.

"Right now, I'm your best freaking friend." She ran her fingers through her ponytail. "And if you want to keep me that way, you'll tell me what I want to know."

"Kaylee, she's really good," Hadley said. "I'd trust her if I were you."

"I'm sure she is, but my father's dead..." she

fought to compose herself. "I don't even know where or how to bury him."

"His wishes are all right here." Hadley handed her a piece of paper. "Pretty detailed." Hadley gave her a sympathetic smile.

Kaylee knew a thing or two about hiding things, and she got the distinct impression Hadley had a few secrets of his own.

"I can only help you if you tell me everything leading up to your return." Emma took her pad and slipped it back in her briefcase, then pulled out a card and handed it to Kaylee. "My cell. Call me day or night, but make sure it's before you talk to Blaine. In the meantime, I want you to map out everything about your life and movements over the last six months, including the details about your attacker. You don't have to give them to me right now, but I want you to do it in the next twenty-four hours." She gave Kaylee a warm smile.

"It's not going to help," Kaylee said.

"I know there's something that you don't want me, or Blaine, or whoever to know. Honestly, I don't give a shit, but if you get arrested, and I have to defend you—"

"You don't have to do anything." Kaylee turned

and stared back out the window. "I haven't even hired you."

"Well, I'd want to. I highly doubt you killed Rutherford, but I can't defend you unless I know everything. And I need to know it before Blaine does. Anything you say or do, he can use against you."

"Basically, I tell you my dirty little secrets, and you'll protect me from the long arm of the law."

"That's what I get paid to do." Emma stuck her hand out.

Kaylee glanced down at the steady hand with the uncontrollable urge to slap it away. Yet, at the same time, she felt a kinship toward this woman, a sense of companionship that infuriated and comforted her.

Grasping Emma's hand in a firm shake, almost trying to hurt the woman, she said, "Deal." Kaylee wanted to feel like she'd just sold herself to the devil, but instead she felt relief.

The sharp jab Blaine felt stabbing into his brain had become increasingly unbearable. The medication could only do so much, and he had little time left before he'd be rendered useless. He glanced at his watch on his way out of his office.

"You okay?" Dave asked.

"I will be when this day is over."

"You can go home. We really don't have enough to make any kind of arrest, so we can continue the interview later."

Blaine closed his eyes briefly, catching his breath and gaining focus. "I'll take you up on that."

"As long as you let Kaylee drive." A firm, fatherly hand squeezed his shoulder. "Speaking of her."

Blaine peeked open his eyes, the bright lights almost blinding him as the bile in his stomach flew up his throat.

"We have unidentified fingerprints on the staircase, the front door, and in the kitchen. I didn't want to say that in there with a defense attorney."

"I take it they're all the same print?"

Dave nodded. "None of which match Kaylee. Her gun is clean, but that doesn't mean anything because Rutherford's wasn't. It appears whoever shot him, may have used his gun."

"Her whereabouts the week before his death are sketchy, but I still can't believe she'd kill him, even unintentionally." Blaine swallowed.

"Until we have a better suspect, I want you to keep a close eye on her. I want her to take a lie detector test, too, but you've got to let me or Williams do most of this. You can always be present, but you can't lead the questions."

"It just kind of started."

Dave's brow shot up. "Don't let it happen again."

Blaine nodded. "What kind of crazy, sick game was Rutherford playing by saying if she didn't want the house, that I got it?"

"That is bizarre. Then again, Rutherford's behavior has always been a bit eccentric."

"Wonder what happened between him and Jack Hicks."

"I heard they had a fight, but I didn't pay much attention." Dave rubbed his jaw. "Does Kaylee have any idea who her biological father is?"

Ignoring the spots dancing about the hallway, Blaine focused on Dave and his words. "Not to my knowledge. There have been so many rumors over the years, most of them suggesting that half this town slept with her mother."

"I think that's the half we start with. And Hadley's sitting in your office."

"Shit. I thought you said I could go home."

"Just ask him. I'll get Kaylee a cup of coffee and see what I can dig up. Did you know Emma's been hanging out with my son, Toby?"

"I know she's hired him a few times." Blaine blinked, trying to keep the inevitable from happening.

"Toby's been acting weird lately."

"He's been busy."

"It seems he's been a homebody, or at least that's what all the bartenders are telling me." Dave stared up at the ceiling, obviously thinking about something besides his wayward son.

"What now?"

"It's about your mother."

"Oh, no. You're joking, right? You want to talk to me about my mother and her love life? Now?" It wasn't like he hadn't seen the way Dave had been looking at his mother over the last few months. Hell, they were both widowed and about the same age. "You've got some balls."

"I guess this is the wrong time, huh?"

Blaine wanted to shake his head, but it would hurt too much. "You want to take my mother out, ask her; don't come to me."

"So, I have your blessing?"

"Christ, get the hell out of my way." Blaine took careful steps back to the office.

"Emma. Dave would like a word with you and Kaylee," he said softly as he walked into his office.

Emma snagged her briefcase, giving him that same cold stare she'd given him the last time they'd crossed paths.

"Kaylee, let's go," Emma said.

"Don't go far." Blaine kept his gaze on Kaylee.

"She doesn't talk to you without me," Emma said. "She doesn't talk to you period."

"This has nothing to do with the case," Blaine said, keeping his gaze locked with Kaylee's.

"Don't care," Emma said and left. Kaylee followed Emma and Hadley set off for the door.

"I need a word with you," Blaine said, bracing himself against his desk.

"I thought so." He turned and plopped himself in one of the chairs. "Ask away."

Blaine took a moment and settled himself in his chair, trying to clear his head, although it felt like a bomb had exploded between his ears. "Did you have an affair with Roberta Mead?" he asked, not going through any of the standard lead-in questions.

"I had a relationship with Roberta Wilson."

"What the hell does that mean?"

"We dated, but then she hooked up with Rutherford."

Blaine wasn't completely incapacitated yet. He considered himself a good judge of character, and Hadley Danks was lying. "So, you never slept with her after she married Rutherford?"

Hadley let out a chuckle. "I might be somewhat of a ladies' man, but I don't go after 'taken' property."

"That doesn't answer my question."

"Look, I know what you're getting at, so let's just cut to the chase. I'm not Kaylee's father."

"How do you know? They got married because Roberta was pregnant." Blaine didn't move a muscle, but Hadley shifted.

"So did Jack and Linda Hicks, but no one ever talks about them, God forbid. If you must know, Roberta didn't want me, she wanted Rutherford, and she made that clear the day she married him."

"Are you sure you're not Kaylee's father?"

"She'd had to have been pregnant for about eleven months for me to be Kaylee's father," Hadley said.

"Any idea who it could be?" Blaine asked.

"Are you suggesting that whoever killed Rutherford could be Kaylee's biological father?"

"Not suggesting anything, just trying to investigate a murder."

"Damn." Hadley rose and rubbed a hand across his face. "Rutherford never really talked about Kaylee's paternity. He never wanted anyone to know."

"Do you know when he found out for sure?"

"When she was about six and got real sick. Something about learning their blood types weren't compatible and he couldn't be her father."

The spots dancing about the room intensified. Blaine took a deep breath and blinked twice. "Can you give me a list of anyone who might have had an affair with Mrs. Mead?"

Hadley nodded. "It'll be a long list, and please don't show it to Kaylee. I'm not sure she'd understand why some people would take advantage of a woman they knew was mentally incapacitated." Hadley gathered his things. "Kaylee's been like a niece to me, and I don't think she needs that kind of pain in her life right now."

The room spun when he took a tentative step on his wobbling legs. "She used to worry she'd end up just like her mother."

"Schizophrenia is hereditary, but from what I've read, the loss of a child would've been a trigger for Kaylee. She seems fine to me," Hadley said.

"I'll be in touch." Blaine pointed to the door and kept his feet moving toward the bathroom down the hallway. "See you later." It seemed all the medication ever did was buy him some time.

After locking the bathroom door, he flicked the lights off and let his stomach empty its contents into the toilet. When the heaving stopped, he braced himself against the sink, taking in slow, calculated breaths. Cold sweat broke out around his hairline, and his body shook. A knock came at the door.

"Blaine? You in there?" Kaylee asked.

"Seriously? You know I have a migraine," he muttered, finding a stick of gum in his pocket. "Grab my keys and meet me at the front door."

"You sure?" Her voice was soft like an angel's.

"Just do it, please." He stiffened his back and rolled his neck. The lights waiting on the other side of the door would hurt, but he'd be home soon enough.

Holding his head high, he managed to make it through the station without too many gawks and stares. Suffering from migraines had always made him feel weak, but he did pride himself that not many people knew he got them. Or how bad they were.

Kaylee was waiting just outside the station.

"My truck." He slipped his dark sunglasses on. They didn't really keep the sun out, but it was better than nothing. "Just take me home so I can sleep this off."

Kaylee struck a match, then lit everything she could find in Blaine's room that resembled a candle or incense. She never thought these types of remedies did anything other than smell like a mix of pine and smoke, but if he thought it would ease his discomfort, well, she'd light the house on fire.

"Thanks," he mumbled when he slipped off his boots and pulled the covers over his bare chest. The lines on his usually flawless face looked as if someone had etched them with a small, sharp object. He curled himself on his side; his eyes were closed, but he didn't look peaceful.

She eased her way down the staircase, pausing at the third step from the top. A lump caught in her throat as she raised her hands to her stomach. The memories of falling and feeling like something had ripped apart inside overwhelmed her.

"Deslin," she whispered, remembering his faint cry. His tiny hand could barely grasp her finger as he struggled to breathe. There was nothing anyone could do to save him, but the doctors were wrong about the pain. It never went away, and it didn't get any better.

Once in the kitchen, she got herself a soda, made a light sandwich, and decided to sit on the porch. The sun had crept behind the mountaintops, creating an orange glow in the sky. It was cool, but somehow her body had become numb to it.

Knowing Blaine could be out for the night, she figured she might as well map out her life over the last few weeks, leaving names out, of course. The name Nino De Luca probably didn't mean anything to the average citizen of Thief Lake, but a hotshot lawyer would probably know of him, or at least his family.

A horn honked just as a red BMW convertible pulled into the driveway. Kaylee set her dishes aside, trying to put a pleasant smile on her face.

Rachael Hicks waved frantically as if they were long, lost sisters. In a way, they were. Rachael wore dark-green slacks, a nice off-white blouse, and her hair flowed straight to her shoulders. Rachael had always had impeccable taste, going with what was in style.

Kaylee glanced at the fancy car. Didn't Rachael know that convertibles were supposed to be driven in the summer, not days where snow loomed overhead?

"Kaylee!" She bolted from the car, but she closed the door like it was her little baby. At least she knew how to treat the car. "I couldn't believe you were here! And oh, God, I'm so sorry."

"Shhh, Blaine's sleeping." Kaylee met her halfway down the stairs with open arms. Kaylee never understood her connection with Rachael. It seemed no matter how hard they tried to piss each other off when they were kids, they always remained friends.

"Sleeping? Why the hell would he be sleeping? He's got a killer to catch. God, I can't believe someone would want to kill Ruther...your dad." Rachael's dramatics hadn't changed one bit. Her face contorted, and she wrinkled her nose like this was the end of the world.

"Maybe because he's been up trying to find out who killed my father since it happened." Kaylee wanted to laugh out loud when Rachael's mouth opened, but no words came out.

"Can't we go in and talk? I'll be quiet."

"You don't know how to be quiet." Kaylee laughed, like they'd been heaved back in time.

Just then Shima walked out on the patio. "Hi, Rachael. How are you this afternoon?"

"Hi, Mrs. Walker." Rachael waved politely. "I'm good, and you?"

"I'll be better when I know we are all safe again. I just spoke with Police Chief Whitcomb." Shima glided across the yard, dangling her keys in hand. "I understand Blaine had a long few days and is probably worn out. Why don't you girls go talk in the house? I've got to run out for a bit."

"Are you sure?" Kaylee asked. It would be nice to catch up with someone who wouldn't drill her with accusatory questions.

"Oh, thank you." Rachael took Kaylee's arm. "It's been so long since we've seen each other."

"You two have a nice night, just lock up when you're done." Shima slipped into her vehicle.

"Oh, where do I begin?" Rachael started as she pulled Kaylee toward the house. "What brought you back here?"

"My father and I decided it was time to mend the fence."

"Really? My dad didn't think your father would ever forgive you."

"Forgive me for what?" Kaylee stopped on the back deck and stared at Rachael. "If this is going to be about bashing Blaine or about the fact my dad wasn't my biological father—"

"I'm sorry. I shouldn't have said that, but you did hurt your dad when you got pregnant and chose to marry Blaine, forgoing college. It's such a nice night; let's sit out here." Rachael always said the wrong thing at the wrong time, but she meant well.

Kaylee sighed, then pulled out a chair and sat down, staring at the moon dancing in the darkening sky. "There's a lot more to it than me and college. Dad didn't like me questioning him about my birth father. He tried to pretend it never came out."

Rachael plopped herself back in a chair next to Kaylee. "Can you blame him?"

"Yeah, I can. I told him it wouldn't change me being his daughter, but he was too stubborn and too damn proud." Kaylee brushed her hair behind her shoulders, but the wind swished it back.

"Sounds like someone else I know." Rachael tilted her head.

"Oh, you're one to talk. You didn't speak to me for a whole month when I started dating Blaine."

"You're absolutely right, and I'm sorry." Rachael looked Kaylee directly in the eye. "But I was sixteen, and I'd told you that I liked him."

"I can't believe we're rehashing this." Kaylee laughed.

"I'm long over it. I'm just so happy to see you."

"Me, too." Kaylee took Rachael's hand in hers. "So tell me, what are you doing these days?"

"You know how much I like to talk about myself." Rachael smiled.

"So, start bragging."

"Let's see...I've started my own little antique shop outside of town, and I'm dating this wonderfully handsome businessman from St. Paul."

"Isn't that kind of far?"

"The relationship is still new."

"How long have you been seeing him?" It felt so good to talk about things other than the mob or a murder.

"Just a few months, but I really think this is the man for me. I'd even move the shop if he wanted me to."

"I hope you get everything you want." All Kaylee wanted was a chance to turn her life around, a chance to get out from under every single mistake she'd made. But right now, she wasn't sure that was going to be possible.

"Does Blaine have any leads?" Rachael asked.

"I'm sure he does, but he's got to keep all that stuff to himself." No point in blabbing she was suspect number one.

"So, tell me. How is the dark man? Picking up where you left off?"

"Please, Rachael. There is nothing to pick up. Besides, I'm outta here as soon as I can clear up my father's estate."

"I see." Rachael sat up straighter. "Thought maybe you'd stick around for a while."

"I'm sorry." Kaylee shook her head. "I didn't mean to snap at you."

"You've never dealt with what happened between you and Blaine." Rachael pointed a finger at Kaylee. "And don't try and tell me otherwise."

"Blaine and I were a long time ago." Even if Blaine did still care for her, he'd never be able to see past her relationship with the mob.

5

The smell of burning wood filled Blaine's nostrils, immediately soothing the dull pain still throbbing in his head, though nowhere near as bad as before. Careful not to disturb the already shaky balance in his system, he shifted to his back and then rolled his legs to the side of the bed.

He sat up, rubbing his temples. The headache would linger, and he'd be sensitive to light for the next few hours, but he knew he was well on the road to recovery because his stomach growled.

The clock he'd made in woodshop class as a teenager said it was after ten. The clock had been the first of many projects in crafting and building that won him a few awards and got him attention with some prestigious schools. Regardless of how talented he was, his heart belonged to protecting the people of this fine community.

He flicked on the reading lamp next to his bed, found a ponytail holder, and slicked back his hair. With his hands on the railing, he leaned over to look down at the family room.

"Kaylee?" He scanned the room, but there was no sign of her. "Kaylee? Where are you?" he called again. "Damn you," he muttered. It would be just like her to run out while he was sleeping. It wasn't like she hadn't done that before.

When he heard an engine roar to life, he raced down the stairs and headed for the front door. As soon as he opened it, the bright lights from the car below momentarily blinded him, sending a sharp pain through his skull. When he got his hands on her, he'd wring her pretty little neck.

"Hi, Blaine," an annoyingly familiar voice rang out.

He squinted, holding his forearm out in front of his eyes, trying to block the light. "Rachael? Turn the high beams off."

He adjusted his vision once again, and a cool breeze kicked up, drawing his attention to the blonde hair flying in the wind. "There you are. I thought maybe you might be trying to run out again."

A look of disgust quickly replaced the semi-smiles he'd been presented with moments ago. "Believe me, the thought has crossed my mind."

"If she goes with you, I could arrest you for aiding and abetting." Blaine waved his finger at a wide-eyed Rachael, who gasped.

"Kaylee, what's he babbling about?" Rachael asked.

"He thinks I killed my father," Kaylee said, deciding the entire town would find out soon enough anyway.

"That's not what I implied, but we do have to cover every angle. And you!" He pointed his finger at Rachael. "Will not repeat any of this conversation to anyone if you know what's good for you." The last thing he needed were certain members of this town accusing him of mishandling this case. "Gossip doesn't solve crimes, only leads to more of them."

"Don't worry," Rachael said, but turned her attention to Kaylee. "You call me if you need anything, okay? I'll always be there for you."

Kaylee smiled and waved as Rachael's bright-red convertible made a left hand turn out of the driveway. She took three stairs up toward the garage apartment.

"Kaylee," he called softly.

She glared at him. "You had no right to talk to her like that."

"Sorry," he said. "Why did she come here?"

"Because she's my friend." Kaylee raised her foot, but paused mid-step when a car revved down the road.

"I thought you might have tak…" He watched a car whiz by, then skid to a halt and back up. "What the?" Blaine took a few steps toward her and squinted, noticing a shiny metal object sticking out of the window. "Get down!" he yelled as he lunged down the stairs toward a stunned, panic-stricken Kaylee. "Now!" He collided with her at the same moment three consecutive pops rang out in the night.

"Blaine?" Kaylee tucked her head in the crook of his neck, while her trembling arms wrapped around him as he lay on top of her.

"Go, Go!" a man yelled. Tires screeched on the pavement as the car sped off.

For a long moment, Blaine lay there, covering her body with his, while he held his breath until he was sure whoever had shot at them wasn't coming back. A slow burn followed by a dull ache in his upper arm forced him to adjust his body to the side.

"You're hurting me," Kaylee whispered. Her warm breath came in short pants against his skin.

"Are you okay?" Alarm burst through his veins. He'd felt the ground vibrate from one bullet, not to mention the second one grazing his arm. "Lay still," he said as he began checking her body for wounds. "Do you hurt anywhere?"

"I'm fine, I think." She brushed hair from her face. "That was just backfire? Right?" Dirt was smudged on her face, and a purplish bruise was forming underneath her left eye.

"I'm sorry," he said quietly, brushing his fingers across her cheek. "That wasn't backfire."

"I didn't think so."

"Go up to the house and hit star one on the phone, that's Dave's line. Tell him what happened and that I need him here." He helped her to her feet, making sure she wasn't hurt.

"Blaine, you're bleeding."

He glanced at the small wound on his forearm. "Must have happened when I jumped you." Wiping a small drop of blood away, he gave her a gentle nudge toward the house. "Go call Dave, please."

She nodded and scrambled up the stairs, both

her hands fisted at her lower back. Blaine grabbed a flashlight from the garage and started looking for the bullets. When the door clanked closed, he glanced at the garage apartment. *What are you running from this time?*

He forced himself to focus. There were three bullets in his yard somewhere, and he intended to find at least one of them. The cold, snowy muck squished beneath his bare feet as he moved methodically across the ground.

"Dave's on his way. Can I help?" Kaylee's voice sang out.

He shifted his gaze toward the steps where Kaylee stood on the landing, arms crossed around her middle.

"You can make me an egg sandwich. I'm famished." For as long as they were together, she'd made fun of his inability to go without food for more than a few minutes. He hoped that giving her a mission to complete would take her mind off knowing someone had tried to kill her, because no one he knew of had reason to be shooting at him.

"You need some aspirin or something?"

He stared at the beautiful woman standing under the bright, starry sky with her hair gently blowing in the night breeze. She could still take his breath away.

"You okay?" she asked.

"Yes," he replied. "Egg sandwich, please?" His chest tightened as she turned away. That woman knew how to sucker-punch him without doing one damn thing.

The sound of an engine coming down the street prickled his ears. He reached behind his back for his weapon. It wasn't there. On tiptoe, he leaped behind the large tree just to the side of the garage.

An orange light filtered through the trees, then white lights turned into the driveway, and Blaine let out his breath as his mother's car pulled in. He moved to the middle of the driveway and pointed to the front lawn, knowing the bullets couldn't have gone in that direction. Dave's pickup followed behind.

"Blaine!" Shima charged from the car. "Dave said you were shot at. Are you okay?"

"When did you talk to Dave?" he asked, glancing over his mother's shoulder.

"I happened to be having coffee with him when Kaylee called." She met his gaze head on.

"I see." Blaine eyed his boss, who just smiled at him.

"Where's Kaylee? She's all right, isn't she?" His mother pursed her lips, like she always did when she got worried about those she cared for.

"She's making me a sandwich."

"I'm amazed at the times you're capable of eating." Dave stood next to Blaine's mother, his hand poorly hidden behind her back. "Dave, would you like a sandwich?" Shima asked.

"I don't think he would," Blaine said quietly.

"Blaine Dakota Walker, you behave yourself."

"I think you're the one who needs to behave," he whispered.

His mother glared at him.

"Do you want a sandwich, Boss?" Blaine was just busting his boss's ass, but his mother didn't seem to be enjoying the poke.

"Actually, I wouldn't mind one. Thank you." Dave flashed a wicked grin, and then kissed her cheek.

Blaine watched Dave eye his mother as she made her way up the stairs to his apartment.

"That's my mother."

"She's also a beautiful woman."

"You don't deserve a woman like my mother."

"I won't argue with that." Dave pulled out a flashlight. "You check out the tire marks?"

"Not yet, still looking for the bullets."

Dave rubbed his jaw. "You're just busting my chops when it comes to Shima, right? Or do you really have a problem with me dating her?"

Blaine continued to scan the ground where he thought the shots might have hit. "It doesn't bother me."

"I never thought I'd look at another woman and not feel like I was cheating on Sally, but your mother makes me think otherwise."

"I'm happy to see her living her life again, but I never thought about her dating. I mean, it's just weird."

"Her dating? Or her dating me?" Dave placed a firm hand on Blaine's shoulder. "We've been friends for years."

"Yeah, and with my dad, too." Blaine's chest tightened. He'd never really had the chance to make his father proud of him.

Dave lowered his stare, his tone level but laced with emotion. "He was one of the best men I've ever known. If he or Sally were still here, we wouldn't be having this conversation."

"That doesn't make it less weirder."

"I know. Shima and I have had the same

conversation. For months." Dave dropped his hand. "I like your mother."

"I can see that." Blaine smacked the flashlight against his palm.

"I'd like you to be okay with this." Dave flashed his own light against the ground.

Blaine felt close to Dave. He'd known him most of his life. Dave was a good man. "I'm sure I'll get used to it." Blaine lifted his flashlight and aimed it right at Dave's eyes. "But if you hurt her, you'll have to answer to me, got it?"

Dave covered his face with his forearm, blocking the hurtful beam of light from his eyes. "Yeah, I got it. Now get back to work before I have to fire your ass."

"It's my night off."

"Not when someone shoots at you."

Blaine knelt down beside a shiny object. "I got a winner." He took the bag and gloves Dave offered. "I'd like to get some pictures of that tread and try to match it."

"Already on it." Dave pulled out a camera bag from the back seat of his pickup. "And once again, you're ruining my night, and you weren't even on the night shift." Dave took a few pictures. "I'll get these out first thing." He tossed the camera in the back of his pickup.

"I think I'm going to call Toby and have him keep an eye on Kaylee while I'm at work." Blaine ripped off the latex glove, tossing it in the wastebasket in the garage before closing it for the night.

"When you do, tell that lazy bastard to stop by and see his old man."

"Why don't you come up and get that sandwich," Blaine offered.

"Thanks."

His mom opened the door with a plate full of food wrapped in foil. "I think Kaylee's tired. She needs her sleep, and I offered the spare, but she insists on staying on your couch." His mother waved a finger under his nose.

"I'll make sure she gets the bed," Blaine said. He leaned in to give his mom a kiss and whispered, "Dave's a good man."

She smiled. "Good night."

"Lock the doors and set the alarm," Blaine said.

"I'll call Jonesy and have him plant himself near here for the night," Dave said as he looped his arm around Blaine's mother.

"Good idea." Blaine watched his mother and

Dave glide arm in arm across the lawn and then disappear into the house before turning and closing his own door behind him.

"They make a cute couple." Kaylee smiled as she put a plate on the counter.

"Oh, yeah, real cute."

"They both deserve some happiness, and they're still so young."

"I know. It's just my boss and my mother and I've known him forever." He'd seen Dave go out on a few dates in the last few months, but nothing substantial, and he hadn't known his mother even looked at the opposite sex. "But hey, if she's happy, I'm happy."

"Toss me a towel." He pointed to his wet muddy feet.

She did as instructed. "I can't believe you're not frozen."

As he wiped the dirt off his skin, he realized he hadn't even buttoned his pants or put on a shirt.

"I must be a vampire," he said, looking across the room at a vision of pure beauty. She'd always had an ease about her, and he could tell that someone had chiseled away some of her resolve, but he was impressed at how she tried to cover it up.

"Can I ask you a tough question?"

She laughed. "Like you haven't been doing that for two days."

"Do you have any idea who your father could be?"

"Any man in this godforsaken town. My father said that Mom had shown some signs of schizophrenia before she got pregnant." Kaylee slammed a cup of juice on the table, and the orange liquid sloshed onto the counter. "You think my biological father wants me dead?"

"I don't know, but something doesn't add up here." He held her gaze for a long moment. "Tell me something that can help you. Something that can push me and my office in a direction that doesn't include you as a suspect."

She leaned against the high-back chair at the counter. "I'm broke, unemployed, and my ex-boss is a number one asshole, but I'm not sure that helps."

"What really happened to you? Who gave you those scars on your back?"

"I already told you."

"No, you didn't." He kept his anger and frustration in check. One thing he knew for sure, Kaylee, if backed into a corner, would fight her way out, but if he did that, she'd never tell him what he needed to know. "You said you were attacked."

"I can't tell you this."

He studied her face. When they'd first fallen in love, he could read her every emotion. Then she got pregnant and the world decided to interfere, and she learned to cover her emotions. Hide them even from him.

All he saw in her face was determination and perhaps a bit of fear.

"If I really thought you killed your father, you wouldn't be in my house. Around my mother. If Dave thought—"

"I get it, but I still can't tell you."

Blaine let out a long, slow breath as he bridged the gap between them. "We once loved each other. We shared joy, and we shared pain. We might not have been able to make things work after we lost our baby, but I'm on your side. I always will be, no matter what."

"No matter how bad?"

"Tell me," he demanded.

"I worked for a lawyer whose clientele consisted of criminals. The mob to be exact."

"One of his clients did this to you?" He ran his fingers across her cheek. She stiffened and pulled away from him. "I can't figure this out and protect you if you're going to keep things from me."

"The man who attacked me said it was a warning." Her voice trembled, but her resolve held.

"What kind of warning?"

"Shouldn't my lawyer be present?" she said so quietly, he barely heard her.

"If I think you need one, I'll let you know, okay?"

"You expect me to trust you?" Her eyelashes fluttered over her pale-blue eyes.

"I do," he said. "Why were you attacked?" He leaned against the counter and broke off a piece of the egg sandwich and stuffed it in his mouth. His stomach growled even more. He'd missed her cooking.

"According to my boy…boss, the guy was just supposed to threaten me."

"Your boss knew about it?" Blaine asked.

She nodded. "It was a way to get me to go back to him. I was hurt and broke, and he controlled me. So I went back. I played along until I could get away."

"Played along with what?" Blaine dropped his sandwich on the counter. The shock of her tale registering deep in his core.

"Played the part of the devoted secretary until I could safely leave and get home. Dad had promised to help me."

"Jesus, Kaylee." He suddenly lost his appetite. "Name. Give me a name. Tell me who did this to you?"

"De Luca, Nino De Luca."

Blaine rolled the name around in his brain and when he finally connected the dots, he thought he might be sick again. "You mean the De Luca family?"

"See why I didn't want to tell you," she said.

Blaine yanked his hair from the ponytail holder, letting it fall to his shoulders. He turned toward the big picture window that looked over the main house. The dry tree branches in the yard were still, and the world appeared to be calm. "Do you think he'd kill your father to get to you?"

"I...I—"

"Just say it." He hated to be in the dark. When you don't know things because of lies, or the omission of the truth, innocent people died.

"When we divorced, I kept your name. Legally, I'm Kaylee Walker. Nino may not even know my real maiden name, linking me to my father."

"And I'm white." He stepped out onto the porch

and slammed the door. Dave's car was still sitting in the driveway to the main house. Through the window he could see Dave and his mother. Blaine felt trapped. He couldn't leave Kaylee alone, or ask her to leave, but he also couldn't go intrude on his mother and Dave. But he didn't want to go back in the house and continue to say things he'd regret in the morning. The Kaylee he knew was smarter than to become involved with the likes of the De Luca family.

When Blaine had fled his hometown, he thought he was moving toward his future. After he had moved back, he realized his problems had only followed him wherever he went. The same was happening to Kaylee.

Her father had been hurt in so many ways. His wife suffered from a horrible condition that led to sexual misconduct, and his daughter had turned out to be someone else's. Blaine glanced at the sky. "Rutherford, I need your help. Speak to me, old man. Tell me something I don't know."

6

Kaylee stared at Blaine's shirtless back through the window. His dark skin in direct contrast with the bright moon. It had always amazed her that his body was a solid mass of fine sculptured muscle, yet he had the worst eating habits of anyone she'd ever met.

Forcing her gaze from him, she finished doing the dishes and started thinking about what to do next. But the situation seemed hopeless. She knew she needed to run. More like disappear. Otherwise something bad would happen, and it would happen to the wrong people.

Her eyelids drooped and her body ached, demanding a peaceful rest, but tonight she'd sleep on the couch. She wouldn't be beholden to him for anything. She grabbed his sweats and her top and padded to the bathroom.

A shower before bed had become part of her routine, and the hot water helped soothe her cramped muscles. When she stepped out of the bathroom, she saw Blaine, leaning against the front door, his legs crossed at the ankles. Considering his heritage, she couldn't understand why she'd want to throw a cowboy hat on him. But sexy or not, he was dangerous and out of the question. She swallowed, forcing herself to move across the hardwood floor.

"Does De Luca want you dead? Or back?" No mistaking his harsh tone.

"I don't think he cares one way or the other." She tried to shrug it all off as she eased herself onto the couch and succumbed to the comfort of the soft leather.

"Do you trust me?"

"It's not that simple." She wrapped herself in the flannel throw blanket.

"I can't help you unless you fill me in on a few things. Like why would Nino De Luca want to hurt you?"

Because he thinks I belong to him, and he's a psycho. "The longer I worked for him, the more I found out about the criminals he had for clients. And I made the mistake of questioning him."

"What kind of criminals?"

"Mostly the white-collar kind—computer hackers, tax evaders."

The couch shifted when he sat down at the other end. "That doesn't sound like the kind of man who'd come after a secretary with a knife for a warning."

"Doesn't matter what it sounds like, it only matters that whoever shot at me tonight, works for De Luca. So I need to go."

"I'm not letting you go." Blaine arched a brow. "You were more than his secretary."

"Doesn't matter what I was to him. I know things about his business. He doesn't like that."

"Did you take anything from him? Files, reports, a damn pen?" he asked.

"No," she lied.

"He had someone stab you. Knowledge is one thing. Proof is something entirely different."

"I made a mistake by getting involved with my boss, but that was it."

Blaine's already dark eyes turned nearly black. "He had someone stab you. Could have killed you."

He threaded his hand through her hair, focusing on the softness of the strands versus his building anger.

"Let it go." She swatted at his hand. "The guy was just supposed to ransack my apartment. I wasn't even supposed to be there, and when I caught him, I hit him over the head with a frying pan. According to Nino, the guy he hired was just fighting back."

"Stabbing you in the back multiple times is simply fighting back?" The intensity of Blaine's hard-as-stone face brought back those frightening moments. She had thought she was going to die— had almost wished for it. "I saw the scars."

"I don't work for him anymore," she managed under a ragged breath. "And I won't ever go back. Problem solved."

"You know your problems are far from solved or you wouldn't have come back here," he whispered. His gaze dropped to her lips, and he cursed softly. He lifted his hand to her chin and tilted her head before brushing his lips against hers.

"Stop it," she said, bolting from the sofa, then clutching her back. "Shit," she slumped down in pain. "See what you made me do."

"I didn't make you jump," he said as he gently turned her body, then pushed her forward. With both hands, he began the most incredible massage she'd ever had, even from a professional.

"Oh, God."

"Feel good?"

"Unfortunately," she managed between heavy breaths. His touch was too sensual to ignore.

"I'll make some phone calls and bring Toby in. He's a good P.I., and if this guy's around, which by this evening's events I'd say is the case, we'll find out and we'll deal with him."

"Why do you want Toby?"

"I can't be here to protect you and out there trying to find whoever killed your dad."

"Oh." She hated to admit it, but the idea of having someone around, watching her, did make her feel better.

"You've always loved a good backrub," he said, running his fingers down her spine.

"You've always been great with your hands." She laughed, although she didn't want to. She didn't want to remember what it felt like to be loved by Blaine.

"Do you remember the first night we got together in the woods by your house?"

"You asked me to meet you and then I found

you slumped over. I thought you were drunk and that I'd have to carry you home."

"I had a migraine."

"Yeah, well, I was already mad at you."

"Why?" His hands lifted her shirt, smoothing down her spine in a slow, torturous stroke.

"You have any idea what it's like to have the entire town make comments about the size of your boyfriend when you hadn't even had the chance to see it for yourself?" She bit down on her lip. The absurdity of the conversation was almost as funny as his little jaunt about town.

"I lost a bet with Toby. I had to do it."

"That's pathetic."

"It got your attention, didn't it?"

"You had my attention fully clothed."

"I know," he said. "I enjoyed making up."

"That was a long time ago."

"A lifetime ago," he whispered. "You must be tired, and I insist you sleep in the bed."

"I'll be fine on the couch."

She gasped when he lifted her into his arms. "Like I said, you'll take the bed."

"Put me down." She stared into his deep, stubborn eyes. "I won't put you out."

"Okay." He winked.

"I won't sleep with you either."

He climbed the short set of stairs with ease. "That's what you said that night."

"That was different." She pushed back the hair that had fallen in her face when he laid her down.

"How so?"

"Stop flirting with me, okay? This isn't helping me."

He scowled and sat on the edge of the bed. "That night I asked you if you trusted me."

"That's because you wanted to get into my pants." She slapped his bare shoulder, letting her hand linger a moment to feel the rigid, yet supple muscles of his body.

"You wanted it as much as I did."

"And what does that have to do with the cost of rice in China?"

"Did you trust me that night?"

"I slept with you, didn't I?" A brief moment of joy filled her heart, followed by the same sadness that had torn her to pieces the day she'd found that check, and her life had been forever changed. She was sure he was long over her, but it was always nice to dream. Her dreams were all she had left. "That was a beautiful night, but it was a long time ago."

"You cried."

"Don't you know all girls cry the first time? And besides, you cried——"

A large, warm hand covered her mouth. "I did not." His look turned serious.

Her breath hitched. The room still smelled like candles mixed with his hot-blooded manliness, making her dizzy.

His soft lips applied the slightest of pressure against the skin on her neck, but her body begged for more. "Blaine," she whispered, unable to form any more words. She'd never been able to get him out of her mind. The few men she'd been with she'd compared to Blaine on every level, but no one had ever stacked up, so she had simply stopped trying. He took her hands and pressed his warm lips against her palms. "Let me give you a decent massage. Your muscles could use it."

A soft hand rippled across her skin as he helped remove her shirt. The bed shifted and creaked when he climbed in next to her. She stuffed her head under the pillow and prayed she wouldn't cry. "This isn't necessary." The scars on her back were ugly, and she was ashamed of them.

"Just let me help you."

A loud clap, followed by what she figured was him rubbing his hands together frightened her, but then warm pressure began to build on her lower back. His strong hands glided effortlessly across her skin. Across her scars.

"How long were you in the hospital?" His voice was tender, but his hands dug deep into her muscles, finding every knot.

"For a few days. Then, because of some nerve damage, I had some problems walking. I spent about two months going to rehab."

"What does this guy really mean to you?"

There was no way she could miss the disappointment in his tone. His fingers roamed up her spine, across her shoulder blades and then back down again. She couldn't tell him that this man snowed her completely. That she'd fallen for the man she thought Nino was. Not the man he really was.

"I dated him. I worked for him. Other than that, nothing." She stiffened at the feel of his full lips pressing against one of her scars. She took a deep breath and could hear him mumbling something, but she allowed her body to relax so deeply that she prayed she'd be able to fake sleep long enough for him to walk away.

Blaine wrestled with his conscience. Kaylee was vulnerable, too vulnerable. He continued to knead her back, feeling all the nodules that were probably causing her more pain than the injuries themselves.

"Tell me to stop." He continued to kiss her back, and his hands squeezed her wonderfully round behind. "Tell me to leave," he whispered. But she didn't move, didn't say anything.

"I should go," he said, staring at his hands against her skin. His copper complexion against her fair, angel-like color had always affected him in the most primal way.

Letting out an exasperated sigh, he decided he couldn't stand it if she outright hated him in the end for taking advantage of her. It was bad enough that she looked at him with distrust in her eyes.

"Sleep well, Kaylee." He pulled the covers up, and when she didn't shift, didn't make a noise, he realized she was sound asleep.

Their marriage had been good on many levels, most especially sexual. He knew she had loved him and he had loved her, but so many people had interjected their own opinions into their relationship that mistrust always reared its ugly head. Looks like things hadn't changed much.

Careful not to wake her, he blew out the

candles, then left the bed and headed downstairs. Lightning flashed through the window, but there was no rain and only a slight rumble of thunder. Spring in these parts could be hot as a July day or as cold as Christmas. Tonight was kind of in-between.

A beer would relax him and ease his ever-increasing desire for the half-naked woman who'd given him pleasure beyond his wildest fantasies once upon a time. So a beer it was.

He sat on the lonely couch, listening to the late show, and then reached for his phone. No time like the present to get a hold of Toby.

"Hello," a familiar female voice said.

"I must have dialed the wrong number, sorry." Blaine glanced at the caller ID, but it most definitely said Toby Whitcomb.

"You didn't dial the wrong number."

"Emma?" he questioned.

"What?" she asked.

He let out a chuckle; those two deserved each other. "Did I interrupt something?"

She sighed. "Do you want to talk to Toby?"

"Yeah." He pinched the bridge of his nose. "You do know what type of guy Toby is, don't you?"

"Oh yeah, I know." Her voice sounded soft and

endearing, but not toward Blaine. "Toby, it's Blaine."

"Yo, Dark Man, what's up?"

"At least I don't glow in the dark," Blaine mused. He'd hated the term "dark man" growing up; now it just made him laugh. "You and Emma?"

"You don't have a problem with that, do ya?"

"Not really, but don't hurt her," Blaine said, hoping she really did know that Toby coined the phrase, 'one-night-stand.'

"Not planning on it. However, you're the one who said you hoped she rotted in hell."

"I was pissed," Blaine said. "How long has this been going on?"

"None of your business."

"Well, I'll be scalped." Blaine ran his hand through his hair. "More than a few days?"

"Try months, man. If you say one jackass thing or tease me at all, I'll do something so bad, you might have to actually put those handcuffs on me."

"I'll leave that privilege for your father, which sort of but not really leads me to why I'm calling."

"Kaylee," Toby said.

Blaine turned the volume on the television all the way down. "Someone shot at her tonight."

"That sucks."

Toby was always one for simple and direct verbiage. "She used to work for Nino De Luca."

"Nino De who?"

"A crime family out of Chicago. Anyway, she's running from something, and I need your help." Blaine scooted down onto his side and propped his head on his elbow.

A belly laugh bellowed in Blaine's ear. "I thought you cops had no use for us low-life P.I. guys."

"I'd like to use your other abilities."

"That's just gross, man."

"Get your head out of your ass. I want to hire you as Kaylee's bodyguard."

"You don't have to hire me to do that." Toby's voice turned serious. "Emma thinks she hiding something, but I haven't been able to get her to break client confidentially whatsoever."

"She never will." Regardless of how horrible their short-lived relationship had been, hating the woman wasn't worth it, and if she made Toby change his stripes, well, more power to her. "Also, since you'll just be hanging around watching, maybe you could do some digging. See what you can find out about what Kaylee has been doing for the last ten years."

"You really want me to open that can of worms?"

"I need to know." Blaine paused for a moment. "And make sure nothing happens to Kaylee, okay? I've got a bad feeling about this."

"Not a problem. Look, I've got a beautiful woman getting naked in my bed. I'm hanging up now."

Blaine wasn't going to comment on that. He shut the phone and glanced toward the window. "Everybody's getting some but me," he groaned and then pulled the covers up to his chin.

When Blaine had left for work the next morning, thankfully, Dave's car had been gone. He didn't think he'd be able to handle a smile on his boss's face as he came out of his mother's house, but he didn't begrudge the man either. Actually, he did. He begrudged anyone who had a sex life.

The sun shone brightly through his half-opened blinds at the station house. There had been frost on the ground, and the weatherman were calling for snow. In the distance, he could see dark clouds rolling in.

A tap at his door caught his attention. His boss leaned against the doorjamb.

"Got some good news for me?" Blaine asked Dave.

"The ballistics on the bullet found at your place didn't match Rutherford's gun," Dave said.

"Did the medical examiner release the body?"

Dave nodded and said, "He died from trauma to the head. If it wasn't for the bullet, they'd rule it accidental. They're supposed to contact Kaylee and Hadley this morning."

"Toby's going to keep an eye on her."

"Good," Dave said. "She tell you anything noteworthy?"

"Not much, but she's definitely hiding something."

"You can say that again." Dave glanced around the office as an uncomfortable silence overtook them. In all the years Blaine had known Dave, they'd never been awkward with each other. Until today. "I need to talk to you."

"Save it, Dave. If you make my mother happy, then I'm happy." He was in no mood for a big talk about them being grown-ups and having so much in common. He might begin to despise the man if he had to go through that.

"I hope I make her happy. I'm in love with her, but that's not what this is about." Dave handed him a file. "Kaylee was engaged to this De Luca guy. He tried to file a missing person's report, but when the cops went to her apartment, they found she'd ended her lease, packed up all her stuff, and told neighbors she was moving to New York. She's not considered a missing person, but Nino's got money. Lots of money. Lots of connections."

Blaine opened the file. A paper clipping of Nino De Luca and his happy fiancée, Kaylee Walker, stared back at him. She really had never changed her name back. He wasn't sure if he was happy about that. Or resentful that she had his name while engaged to another man.

"She did tell me she was involved with him," he said as he flipped through more clippings. "But not this involved."

When he got to the one where she'd been attacked by a burglar, he pounded his fist on the desk. "She told me the attack was meant as a warning. You should see the scars on her back."

"That is one hell of a warning."

"I asked Toby to do some digging. Mind if I give him all this?"

"Go ahead. All public record."

"What else have you found out?"

"De Luca claims that he thinks Kaylee's attacker might have kidnapped her for ransom or something. He's put out a few press conferences, and I'm sure he's got a bunch of hired hands scouting for her."

Blaine rubbed his hand across the scab forming on his bicep. "I think we met them last night."

Dave took a seat across from Blaine. "Either De Luca put a hit on her father to get to her. Or he was at the right place, but the wrong target. Or, we've got two sets of bad guys here."

Blaine rose and strode to the window. The sun was hiding behind a cloud, and he could hear the wind howling in the distance. Snow was definitely on its way. "I think we really need to cover both angles. If it's Nino, he'll keep coming. If it's someone else, I bet my next paycheck it's related to information regarding her biological father."

"I get the crime family connection, considering she's obviously running from something, but what's the big deal about who her father is anyway?"

"I'm not exactly sure, but what if it's someone whose career or family would be ruined?"

Dave let out a soft roll of laughter. "It's the new millennium; no one gives a shit these days."

Blaine turned to face his boss. "Someone like Reverend Hicks would give a shit."

"You can't be serious? Straight-laced Jack? Come on, Blaine. He'd never cheat on his wife."

"Stranger things have happened."

"I can't let you pursue this. You have nothing to go on and frankly, I think you're just looking for a reason to believe she's not tangled up with the mob."

The sky outside grew dark, and the wind rattled the window. "You have to agree that we need to look at every possible angle."

"That's not the point. Kaylee is still on the suspect list. She has a lot to gain from her father's death, and she was the last to possibly see him alive." Dave let out a huff of air, frustration written all over his face.

"If she's up there, then so is Jack. Maybe he didn't think Rutherford had changed his will just yet. Maybe there was a heated argument and Rutherford threatened to expose Jack's infidelities to his wife. Either way, Jack is out millions for his church. That's motive right there."

"I'll give you the possibility, but damn it, do it by the book."

Blaine knew he couldn't go and speak to them,

officially. "It's been a few months since I've gone to church—"

"Try years, son." Dave shook his head. "Don't give me reason to suspend you."

"Wouldn't dream of it." Blaine had seen that concerned look on his boss's face before. When Blaine had come back and started working for him the second time, Blaine was truly lucky to have a job. No one would hire him because he was a loose cannon ready to blow.

"Just remember who you answer to," Dave said before disappearing into the hallway.

A few things had changed, but Blaine still preferred to bend the rules just a smidgen, just to get the job done. That would never change.

Just then Blaine's cell phone rang. Glancing at it, he saw Toby's number. "What's up?"

"It would appear Kaylee talked Rachael into driving her to the police station." Toby laughed. "She's got an extra key in the tire hub. I'll stop her, but you better get your ugly ass out here." The phone went silent.

The woman was going to make him nuts.

7

K aylee stared out into the evening sky as she listened to a screeching voice lecture her about being on the run from the cops. How it would be better if she just stayed put and let her closest friend and the rest of this sleepy little town help her. Kaylee couldn't believe hiding out with the Assistant Chief of Police was going to protect her from the mob, especially since they already knew where she was hiding.

"Are you listening to me?" Rachael snapped.

"Every flipping word."

"But you're not going to take my advice, are you?" Rachael slammed her car into park and gave Kaylee the evil eye. "You realize you're making yourself look guilty."

"Great, now you believe I killed my father."

Rachael reached out and held Kaylee's forearm. "I don't believe that, but running won't help you. You've got to stop. Even Rutherford was tired of it."

"What do you know about my dad?" Kaylee yanked her arm free and glared at Rachael. "You act like you've talked to him about this."

"I sold him some furniture from my shop a while back. He mentioned how much he missed you. How he wanted you back in his life. He was looking for you."

"My father bought some furniture from you? He was never interested in change." Kaylee blinked. It wasn't the furniture so much as the fact that he'd confide in Rachael. That Rachael would even listen to him. Growing up, Rachael had thought her father a total asshole.

"I worked him over."

"How'd you do that?"

"That's a long story, and I won't be telling it to you unless you show up at my place for dinner one night in the near future."

"Thanks, Rachael, but I'm not staying."

The sun was hidden by dark storm clouds, and the leafless tree branches flapped in the wind. She figured she'd have about a half hour to get back to Blaine's, get her stuff, and head for the hotel. She couldn't stay with Blaine another night. She couldn't put his mother in danger either.

"Thanks, Rachael." Kaylee opened the door to the sports car and stepped onto the pavement.

"At least stay for my parents' annual barbeque. My new boyfriend is going to be there, and I'd love for you to meet him."

Kaylee froze at the mention of the kind Reverend Hicks, who wasn't so kind. He'd always treated her like some kind of heathen or possibly the devil himself. Once, he'd even told her she was just like her mother. Of course, Kaylee had been pregnant and unmarried at the time, which made people wonder if she was schizophrenic.

"Well, lookie at who we have here," Toby's voice rang out.

When she turned, Toby had successfully put his car, if you could call the rusted pile of metal a car, behind her SUV. She was blocked in, and without a doubt, Blaine knew by now she was here.

"Hey, Toby." She scurried over to give him a hug. "Please let me leave," she whispered. "I need to get out of here."

"Damn girl, and to think I'm taken." He squeezed her bottom shamelessly, ignoring her words.

"You're taken? By what?" She cupped his bearded face and narrowed her eyes. Toby had always understood her; she hoped that was still the case.

He smiled and rolled a toothpick sticking out of the side of his mouth with his tongue and shook his head. "No can do, babe." He leaned his broad body against her car. "I think we should all go out tonight."

Rachael cleared her throat.

Toby glanced at her. "Your big-wig boyfriend isn't around, and having five wheels isn't—"

"Well, I never." Rachael huffed and then got back in her car. "Kaylee, call me later, okay?"

Kaylee waved as Rachael drove off. "Toby, that wasn't very nice."

"You skipping out isn't very nice either." A belly roar filled the air. "And after what she did to me, hell and fire." He twiddled his toothpick. "Why would I give her the time of day?"

"What did she do?"

"Forget it. Let's go find the boss."

"Toby?" She hesitated and pulled open the car door. "Please, Toby. Just let me leave."

"I wouldn't help you run back then, what makes you think I'd help you now?" He batted her nose and strutted toward the station house, leaving his rusted Jeep behind her car.

Big, puffy snowflakes began to fall from the sky. The wind died and then swirled in a howl, then softened again. She took in a deep breath of the cold, crisp air.

She eyed Toby's car to see if she might be able to squeeze by, but it didn't look good.

"You're not going anywhere," Blaine yelled. "You ran out on me ten years ago without an explanation, and I won't let you do it to me again." He marched across the pavement. His cowboy boots banged and clanked with each long stride. He wore jeans, a T-shirt, a light jean jacket, and his long, dark hair flowed from his face as he stomped toward her.

She stared at him, knowing her mouth was wide open and she was unable to move, much less breathe. A gasp tickled her throat when she tried to say something—anything—but couldn't.

"You have some explaining to do," he whispered.

Her five-foot-six-inch frame seemed tiny as he towered over her, having at least six or seven inches on her. She locked gazes with his dark, intense stare. "I...I...already explained why I left and where I went."

"Not that." Without warning, he grabbed her hips. "We miscommunicated because people lied to us, but this time you're lying to me." His eyes bore into hers like a tiger ready to pounce. "I can throw you over my shoulder or you can get in the car. Your call."

"You wouldn't dare! Isn't that kidnapping or something?"

"So, call the cops," he said, unlocking his truck. "Get in."

"You can't boss me around—"

"Get in or I'll make you," he said.

She clenched her jaw but complied, knowing he wasn't past tossing her over his shoulder at this point.

"If you think about running, I'll handcuff you."

"You're being an asshole," she said.

"Stop lying to me, and I'll stop being an asshole." He slammed the door shut and then leaped across the truck, uttering numerous curses.

Large drops of snow floated and swirled about in the howling wind. Small, white mounds had already begun to collect on the roads. The truck skidded and fishtailed as he squealed out of the parking lot.

"Stop this truck right now. I refuse to go anywhere with you when you act like this."

"You have to stop running, Kaylee," he said in a soft tone, but his hands gripped the steering wheel, and his eyes focused on the road as he drove way too fast. "You have to start being honest with me."

"I don't have to do anything."

The roads heading out of town and to his house were empty. He took the curves tight and fast. She braced herself as the truck fishtailed again. "Slow down."

She felt the car ease up slightly.

"I'm tired of your bullshit." He took the turn onto Route 5, his house now just a mile down the road. "I know you're in trouble. I know someone is trying to kill you, and I know you're lying to me."

"None of which has anything to do with you."

"It has a lot to do with me." He laughed. "Besides finding you crumpled over your father's body. Besides someone shooting at you in my driveway. You decided to put me in the middle of this."

The truck skidded sideways as he pulled into the driveway.

"You put yourself in the middle of this the moment you brought me back here. Had you let me go to the hotel—"

"You'd be gone. And most likely dead." He shut the engine off. "I'm not going to let someone kill my wife."

"Ex-wife," she corrected him.

"Whatever." He slammed the door and headed for the stairs, leaving her in the truck. "Not so fast." She stepped into the cold night air. "You don't get to dump all that on me and walk away."

He turned and faced her. "Why not? That's what you were going to do to me."

"I didn't dump this on you."

"Fine." He raised his arms, palms facing the sky. "But that doesn't change the situation, and I can't stand by and let someone I care about put themselves in the line of fire, literally." He turned and took the stairs to his apartment two at a time.

The snow had started to fall harder as she made her way up the stairs, leaving her footprints behind. He'd left the door open, but once inside, he didn't talk, didn't look at her, just went for the refrigerator. He got himself a beer, opened it, chugged half of it down, and then sat down on the sofa.

She took off her coat, shaking off the snow. "I didn't mean to drag any of you into this."

"I know," he said. "But we're in it, and it just pisses me off that you don't get I'm on your side. That I want to protect you. Help you."

"It's not that I don't get it," she said. "I'm ashamed."

He closed his eyes for a moment before opening them again and locking gazes with her. "Come here."

"No."

"Why not?"

"I shouldn't be here at all."

He sipped his beer and stared at her. "You can't run out on this," he said. "Not just because of what happened to your father, but because of those scars on your back."

She sat on the edge of the sofa. "It's killing me that I'm putting you in danger."

"You do remember I'm a cop, right?"

She smiled weakly. "Your mother could get caught in the cross fire."

"She has a cop for a son and a cop for a boyfriend. I think she understands the danger."

Blaine had always had an answer for everything. It was difficult to win any argument with him because of that. But also because sometimes he was just right. But in this situation? The De Lucas wouldn't think twice about snapping his mother's neck. Her situation wasn't going to change, and no matter how much she wanted to curl up in his arms, the De Lucas would destroy him and not look back.

"I'd been working on leaving for months. I had to get my back better before I could do that. The longer I stayed, the worse the situation became. And now I just need to hide."

"You can't run," he said. "They will find you." He tugged at her arm, pulling her closer. "Let me protect you." He pressed his lips against her temple. "I'm sorry I blew up at you, it just scares me that you'd be so reckless as to try and do this on your own. Being alone isn't smart."

She relaxed into his body. Her head rested on his shoulders, his arm looped around hers. She lifted her feet, tucking them off to the side. He set his beer down, snagging the remote off the coffee table. He picked a television station with an old sitcom. She didn't really watch it. And he had the volume turned down so low, she could barely hear it anyway. Instead, she contemplated her situation. If she ran, she had to take care of one thing first, and she couldn't do that for a day or two. But Blaine was right. Running could get her killed. Nothing she didn't already know.

But staying could get any number of people killed, including Blaine.

"You're deep in thought." He tugged gently at her hair. "What are you thinking about?"

She sat upright. He had one arm stretched out on the back of the sofa. The other one on the arm rest.

"I bet I know what you're thinking about." He winked.

"Yeah, what's that?"

"You want me."

"Seriously? Not a time to joke around."

"I'm not joking. I can see it in your eyes. They change color when you—"

"That's not true," she said, though this was something he'd constantly told her when they were young and in love.

"It is true. And you want me."

"Anyone ever tell you that you're conceited?"

He nodded. "But I'm right," he said. "You want

me, and I can prove it." He slowly stood, pulling her with him. "No matter how hard you try to deny it, you still want me." His lips hovered over hers. She held her breath as she tried to rid her mind and body of all the things this man could do to her. All the things he could make her feel.

"Blaine—"

His lips brushed against hers. She didn't close her eyes. She couldn't tear her gaze away from his enchanting stare.

"This isn't a good idea," she whispered. His hands were on her hips. His thumbs under her T-shirt, rubbing her bare skin.

"I think it's a great idea." He smiled devilishly.

She tried to wiggle from his grip as she packed herself against the railing to the stairs. "I don't want you." Neither the words nor the tone sounded very convincing.

"Hmm." He looked mildly amused. "That's not what your body says." His eyes glanced below the neckline.

Her nipples tightened. "I'm cold."

"No, you're hot. Probably on fire."

She moaned when his hand cupped the swell of her breast, his thumb fanning over her taut nipple.

With the intention of pushing him away, she

grabbed his wrist, but she just held it there as his forefinger and thumb turned and plucked her nipple.

"Tell me you want me," he whispered.

"I want you," she said. "But—"

"No buts." He kissed her nose, then her cheek. It was tender. Gentle. Then he kissed her mouth. Their tongues met with wild fury like the storm brewing outside. She leaned into his hard chest, ripping his T-shirt from the waistband of his jeans and lifting it over his head, forcing their lips apart. His bare chest raised up and down with a heavy breath. She reached out and ran her hands across his hard stomach muscles. She admired his beautifully sculptured body. Every inch of him was thick and hard. She began to fiddle with the buttons on his jeans. But he stopped her.

Gentle hands lifted her shirt above her head. "So beautiful," he said, tracing a path over the curve of her breast. He found the front clasp of her bra and released her aching mounds.

She couldn't concentrate on anything but his fingers gently tugging at her nipples, his lips on her neck, driving her mad with passion. She closed her eyes and dropped her head back. He gave pleasure to one breast with this hand and the other with his tongue. "Perfect," he said as he knelt down and assaulted her stomach with soft kisses.

He rolled her jeans down, tugging her underwear with them. "Most beautiful woman I've ever seen."

He'd always been one to give her romantic compliments in and out of bed. His lovemaking always made her feel special. She opened her eyes to see him stepping back, staring at her naked body.

"You like what you see?" With him, she'd always felt completely comfortable being sensual. Odd how that seemed to be like riding a bike, because with other men, she'd always felt the need to cover up and hide.

He nodded and pointed to the stairs.

"You first." The wind howled, banging branches against the windows.

"No."

The hardwood floor squeaked when she took a step toward him. His muscles twitched as she ran her hands over his chest.

"Upstairs," he said hoarsely as he laced his fingers through hers. All the way up the stairs, he never once took his eyes off her naked body. Once at the foot of his bed, he gently lifted her off the floor and placed her on the bed. He knelt in front of her. His hands gently spreading her legs and lifting them over his shoulders. She dropped to her elbows, arching her back. His hot breath tickled her right before he pressed his lips against her and his tongue dived into her. She looked down at him. His head buried between her legs. His long, dark hair flowing over her body.

Clutching the comforter, she tried to hold her body as still as she could, savoring every sensation. Every stroke of her insides. His hand moved across her stomach, making its way to her breast. He took her nipple between his finger and thumb, turning the hard flesh left, right, and then tugging it away from her breast. She couldn't take it anymore. She lifted her hips, then pushed down toward the bed. "Please," she begged him, shifting her hips again.

His thumb found her hard, throbbing mound. He fanned it a couple of times, while his tongue still swirled inside her. He lifted his head. His gaze met hers as he slid his fingers inside her, his other thumb still rubbing her. She spread her legs wide, resting her feet on the edge of the bed.

"Ready?" he asked.

She could only nod.

He pinched her hard, swollen nub, then rubbed his thumb over it in a circular motion. His fingers glided in and out of her swiftly and with purpose. He bent his head and replaced his thumb with his tongue, lapping harshly and sucking while his fingers still danced inside.

She fell to her back, clutching her breasts, plucking at her own nipples. She arched her back, moaning. No one had ever been able to make her feel the way he did. She felt him switch from his tongue to his fingers again, tugging and making circular motions until her body quivered. And convulsed. He continued massaging her, but she couldn't take it anymore. She closed her legs tight, holding his hands between her thighs, her stomach muscles still contracting with pleasure.

He kissed her knees than stood, his hands undoing his belt buckle.

"You had your fun," she said. "My turn."

He smiled, dropping his hands, letting her undo his pants. "I'd say you had just a little bit of…" He hissed as she released him, taking the tip into her mouth, swirling her tongue around the edges. She held him with one hand, stroking the base, while she licked and kissed the tip, the sides, then eventually took all she could into her mouth.

He fisted a wad of her hair in his hand and

tugged. She looked up at him, her eyelids heavy. She squeezed his hardness.

"Stop," he said.

"I'd say you're ready."

"Not yet."

After he'd found a condom by his bedside, he settled his broad hips between her parted legs and pushed down in one tortuously slow stroke. He repeated the motion a few times, his arms keeping the weight of his body off hers. He stared into her eyes with such passion and desire. She arched her back, shifting her hips.

"I don't want to hurt your back."

"You're not," she said, grinding her hips frantically against him.

"But I might." He rolled over onto his back, pulling her on top of him.

She let out a small laugh. "You just wanted me on top."

"Well, there is that." His hands encouraged her hips, and she rocked over him, slowly, teasing him, building up her own anticipation. His hands reached up and toyed with her nipples while she rocked back and forth and up and down. She could feel his thigh muscles tighten. His hands dug into her ass, guiding the motion.

She leaned forward, pressing her hands on the bed, angling herself so when she grinded against him, every part of her was touched.

He raised his head and sucked a nipple into his mouth. He sucked hard. His tongue swirling roughly against the sensitive skin. His hands ran from the small of her back to cupping her ass, digging her fingers into her flesh. Her stomach tightened, and wetness poured out of her again, her body shuddering with delight.

Blaine dropped his head. He held her hips still as he moved his until a guttural groan escaped his mouth and he slowed his pace, his hands releasing their tight grip. She dropped her head to his chest. Both gasping to catch their breath. They lay there for a long while. The only noise was their breathing.

"Blaine?"

"What?"

"I'm getting cold."

He gently pushed her aside, arranging the comforter and the sheets so their bodies were covered.

She snuggled into the crook of his shoulder, and he held her close.

"Promise me you're not going to run," he whispered.

"I can't promise," she said. "I don't want to, but I can't promise."

"That's an honest answer." He kissed her temple.

———————

Blaine held Kaylee in his arms, knowing nothing had changed. He'd like nothing more than to hide out in his tiny apartment and make love to her over and over again, but that wouldn't do either one of them any good. He had to first find out who had killed her father, while protecting her from the mob.

A humming noise followed by his nightstand vibrating snapped him from his trance. He snagged his cell phone and flipped it open.

"Hello" he said, not letting Kaylee go as she tried to slip from his grasp.

"Blaine, it's Hadley."

"What can I do for you?"

"I need to talk to you and Kaylee about Rutherford."

Blaine kissed her softly on the forehead. "Okay."

"In person. Is she there?"

"Yes."

"I'll be over shortly." The phone went dead.

Blaine dropped the cell to the floor. "We're going to have company soon." He shifted the covers, giving him better access to her naked body.

"What are you doing?"

"What does it feel like I'm doing?" Her skin was still beaded with sweat from their last encounter, but he hadn't had enough of her yet. He ripped the covers off their bodies altogether.

She reached for the blankets. "It's cold."

"Let me warm you up."

She'd always been the most beautiful creature he'd ever seen.

"Who's coming here?" she asked.

"Who cares?" he said, as headlights beamed through the window. "Hadley wasn't kidding when he said he'd be right over."

"Oh, great." Kaylee gathered up the sheet, wrapped it around herself and started searching the room. "My clothes are downstairs."

"I'll get them for you," he said, hiking up his jeans.

"You don't think he could be my father, do you?"

"He says it's impossible." Blaine gave her an apologetic smile. He wondered who else she thought could be her father and what she'd think about his theory. "I asked him to compile a list."

"That would be unpleasant to look at," she mumbled and then hauled ass to the bathroom, sheet and all.

Blaine couldn't really fault her for her sentiment. Her mother had suffered from a horrible disease before killing herself. Then Kaylee returned home, landing herself in the middle of her father's murder. Of course, Blaine couldn't forget she was running from some very bad people.

Hadley pounded at the door just as Kaylee stepped from the bathroom. "Hey," Blaine said, opening the door. "Wow, look at that snow."

"Calling for at least twelve inches, maybe more." Hadley dusted the snow off his shoulders as he took a step in. "Where's Dave?" he asked.

Blaine blinked and then glanced out at the driveway. Dave's pickup was parked right next to his. "He's been dating my mother."

"I guess I shouldn't be surprised," Hadley commented. "If you don't mind me saying, your mom's quite a looker."

"So I'm told."

"Hey, Kaylee," Hadley said.

Hadley took out some papers and moved into the galley kitchen. "Got a beer?"

"What's bothering you?" Blaine eyed the man helping himself to a beer. Hadley might have been an old friend, but they certainly weren't that close.

"A lot of things, namely this." He tossed an envelope on the counter. "I've been going through all my files on Rutherford, and I came across an old envelope he'd given me a while back. Honestly, I'd forgotten all about it."

"What is it?"

"A list of people he knew was sleeping with Roberta." Hadley tipped his beer back and swigged.

"I don't think I want to be here for this," Kaylee said.

"You need to hear what I have to say," Hadley said.

Blaine glanced at the envelope. "Why would people sleep with her knowing she was unbalanced?"

"Early on, none of us knew. She'd always been precocious as a teen, and Rutherford knew she had a reputation when he started dating her." Hadley seated himself on the barstool. "Her family was powerful, and I think Rutherford turned a blind eye. Then he just tried to control her actions and keep things under his roof, so to speak."

"When did he give this to you?" Blaine lifted the envelope and carefully pulled out the single piece of paper. He'd always wondered why Rutherford didn't force Roberta to take her medication, or institutionalize her or something.

"I think it was right before she killed herself. Deep down Rutherford really believed he was protecting her. And Kaylee."

"A lot of good that protection has done me over the years." Kaylee sat at the breakfast bar, her arms folded across her chest.

Blaine read over the list. "What do you think?"

"I think Rutherford was a spiteful man." Hadley polished off his beer. "I wonder if he wasn't planning these men's demise."

"Were he and my mom ever happy?"

"Happiness comes in degrees." Hadley rubbed his jaw. "Rutherford wanted a wife from a certain background, a child, and the perfect home. He got more than he bargained for."

"And this is code for what?" Blaine asked

"I'm sorry, Kaylee," Hadley said. "I don't want to hurt you, but your father got what he deserved."

"Now you're the one who sounds bitter." Blaine

folded the paper and set it aside, not wanting Kaylee to see it.

Hadley let out a hearty laugh. "We were like brothers. Sometimes I loved him and other times I wanted to beat the shit out of him."

"Maybe you wanted him dead." Blaine got himself a beer.

"Well, he's driving me nuts, even in death." Hadley ran his hand across his face. "But I should tell you that I lied about something."

"What?" Blaine asked.

"Kaylee, I hope you will be able to forgive me." Hadley stood up, but didn't move.

"For what?"

"You know I had an affair with your mom before she and Rutherford were married, but…well, I slept with her later on, too." Hadley craned his neck. "At one point, I thought I could be your father. But then we all started to realize how sick Roberta really was. She started talking crazy, and I thought it best to leave it alone until after you were born."

"What happened when I was born?" Kaylee asked.

"Your dad really thought you'd make Roberta happy and she'd snap out of it. Then the diagnosis came, and I just couldn't bring myself to tell him about the affair until you got sick."

"I'm confused," Kaylee said. "Are you my biological father? Do you know who my father is?"

Hadley shook his head and tossed another piece of paper on the table.

Blaine moved to stand next to Kaylee and put his arm around her. None of this could be easy for her to hear.

"You were six when you needed a blood transfusion. He wasn't too happy when the doctor told him his blood couldn't help you. Privately, I got tested, but found out it wasn't me either. No one else came forward, though your father privately asked a few people." Hadley looked at Kaylee with guilt and shame in his eyes.

"You all knew since I was six that my dad wasn't my dad?"

Hadley nodded.

"Kaylee got her blood transfusion. Who was the donor?" Blaine asked.

Hadley shrugged. "They had some in the blood bank, and Rutherford begged me to help him keep this whole paternity thing a secret. It didn't come out until Kaylee almost bled to death in childbirth."

Hadley rose from the chair and moved across the room.

"Where did the blood come from after Deslin was born? I had to have a transfusion then too, but I don't remember…" Kaylee's voice shook, and her eyes pleaded with Blaine.

"The hospital had enough of your blood type."

"He looked so hurt when I yelled at him later, calling him a fake," she whispered. "I accused him of using me to not only trap Mom and hold her hostage, but that he'd been the one drugging her and making it look like she was sick."

"Those are your mother's words, not yours, and you'd just been through hell and back. Then to find out your father wasn't really your father, no one could blame you." Blaine tried to comfort her, but he'd failed her ten years ago when he'd chosen not to be there for her. He knew he was too late now. "Hadley, do you think anyone on that list would have a valid reason for killing Rutherford?"

"Valid or logical?"

To a sick individual, the reason wouldn't matter, and Blaine knew that. "Just asking your opinion."

"All of us at one point or another had reason to hate the man, including the two of you."

Blaine really couldn't argue that point, and he didn't want to. "Anything else?"

"All of Rutherford's assets are tied up until his death can be resolved." Hadley rose and walked toward the door. "I'll keep going through my files, but I'd search that house and look for anything he might have kept of your mother's. And that damned room he always bragged about."

"You think my biological father killed him, don't you?" Kaylee followed him to the door.

"Either him, or someone who doesn't want the truth to come out."

"Didn't your mother get into the booze and rant about perverts that would come and rape her?" Blaine asked.

"When she had stopped taking her meds altogether, she'd go nuts, dressing up and trying to sneak out. She'd drink and rant about the men Dad would send to seduce her." Kaylee covered her face and shook her head. "When she got like that, it scared me. I didn't want to end up like her, but the meds made her even more pathetic. She'd sit at the table and color, like a kid."

"She needed help. Help your father should have gotten her." Hadley took Kaylee into his arms. "I should've been a better friend to both of them."

Blaine glanced out into the white of winter, trying to piece together everything he could remember about Mrs. Mead. One thing kept coming to mind: she believed Rutherford was always watching, but never doing anything to help her. She'd even once cornered Blaine, begging him to get her out of the 'house of cameras.'

"Thanks for stopping by." Blaine closed the door after a whoosh of air blew some snow into the house. "I'm hungry. You?" A good mystery always got his stomach going. He'd given up trying not to eat at inappropriate times.

She snapped her head up and glared at him. "You are unbelievable."

"I know this is hard for you, but thus far, you haven't learned anything new."

"Great," she muttered. "And I thought you'd changed."

"I have."

"Not." She flipped on the stove, pulling out a skillet. "Still an insensitive bastard."

"I'm just hungry." He cocked his brow.

"Okay, I get it." She pulled out the eggs. "You're always hungry."

"Sit. I'll cook."

"Works for me," she said.

"Tomorrow we go check out your house, and then on Sunday, we go to church."

"Neither one of us do church, unless—"

"I don't do church, but I have an idea about who your father could be, if you want me to find out."

"I do and I don't, but you seem to think my father's death has to do with whoever my father is and not whoever is trying to kill me ."

"I'm saying it's a possibility." He tossed some bread on the counter. If Nino De Luca wanted her dead, she'd be dead by now. Those men who shot at them could have easily hit their mark. But they didn't. Nino wanted something from her. Something important. "You're not going to like this."

"I don't like anything about being back in this town."

Blaine squeezed the egg in his hand, cracking it. He rinsed his hand in the sink. "You seemed to like what we were doing about an hour ago."

"That was an hour ago."

"Gee, thanks," he said. Stupid to be upset over her sarcasm, but he just wanted an acknowledgement from her that he still mattered. "I'll order a pizza." He grabbed the phone and headed for the door. He was being stupid and childish, but she had the ability to crush his heart. Again.

"Blaine, I—"

"Save it." He slammed the door shut. There he stood in the snow, barefoot, staring down at the sky, sucking the cold air into his lungs.

Life had too many cruel twists, although this had nothing to do with cruel twists, but sheer stupidity on his part. He had only himself to blame. He knew the moment he climbed into bed with her that he'd be the one to suffer the consequences.

8

K AYLEE opened the door and yelled. "Now who's running?" She slammed the door and stared out the window at Blaine's back. He hadn't even turned around. This wasn't about them having sex. This was about her crazy mother and not-so-sane father. This was about her life, her problems, not his stupid ego. He shouldn't take things so damn personally.

She sighed, leaning against the wall. He'd always been the quiet, sensitive type. One of the many things that had drawn her to him. He loved deeply. It was the kind of love you felt through to your soul. It was the kind of love that stayed with you forever. She felt just as connected to him now as she did the day she found out she was carrying his baby. And maybe he felt it, too.

Large snowflakes fell from the sky. The wind swirled and howled, but Blaine didn't even look cold. A shadow by the garage door caught her attention. She opened the door, and this time Blaine turned around.

"I'm sorry," he said.

She stepped in behind him and wrapped her arms around his strong waist, resting her head on his back. "I am too. Who's in the garage?" she asked.

"No one." He leaned over the railing.

A loud swooping noise filled the crisp night air, and wild orange and red lights flickered in the window below. "Is that—"

He pushed her aside as he went into the house. A snowmobile raced across the street and into the driveway. Blaine returned with his weapon in his hand.

"What's going on?" She glanced between the two figures on the snowmobile and Blaine. "Is that Toby?"

"Yes," Blaine said.

Toby waved frantically toward the backyard as a

smaller figure leaped from the moving snowmobile and headed for the garage.

"Go to the main house."

She watched Blaine jog across the yard, his dark hair whipping around wildly as he headed off into the night.

"Kaylee, come on!" his mother yelled.

She stuffed her feet in her shoes and grabbed Blaine's coat, then raced down the stairs. The heat from the fire warmed her skin as she passed the door to the garage.

Dave was running across the yard. "Get inside," he said. "I've called it in." Dave grabbed the hose from the figure in front of the garage. "Go. Get in the house."

But Kaylee couldn't move. She stood in the middle of the driveway, staring at the flames flickering in the night. The person who had jumped off the snowmobile took off their helmet. "Emma? What are you doing here?"

"Came with Toby and we saw the fire and then a figure running out the side door of the garage."

"Come on, girls," Shima yelled. "In the main house. The fire department is on its way."

"Whoever started the fire went that way." Emma pointed through the backyard.

"I bet they trudged through the woods and have a car waiting for them by the interstate," Dave said, doing his best to douse the fire with a small hose.

"Pretty stupid in the snow," Kaylee said, still staring at Emma. Not in a million years would she think that woman would ever wrap her legs around a snowmobile, much less Toby. And the fact Toby was even interested in that type of women? Things sure did change around this town.

"Not if they expected everyone to be asleep, then the snow would cover their tracks by morning." Dave continued to hose down the inside of the garage, specifically Blaine's late-model Mustang.

Kaylee glanced back at the garage. Small flames flickered inside the car, and her nostrils were assaulted with the stench of burning leather. Her pulse slowed to a painful beat.

"Blaine loves that car. This is going to really piss him off," Emma said, looping her arm over Kaylee's shoulder. "Let's get inside. I'm sure there isn't much damage to anything but the Mustang."

"We'd be dead by morning," Kaylee barely managed behind the constriction of her throat muscles.

"That might have been the point," Dave added.

Kaylee shuddered, wrapping her arms around her middle. "I have to get out of here."

"No, you don't," Emma said.

"You don't understand. As long as I'm here, everyone is in danger."

Emma nudged her up onto the porch. "You've got the best two cops in the county, the best P.I., and, if you need me, the best legal representation. We've got your back."

"Really. You don't understand." Kaylee shrugged her arm off. She stomped the snow off her shoes and entered the kitchen. She headed straight for the bathroom. Her stomach swished and gurgled.

The small bathroom smelled like lilacs and vanilla. She inhaled sharply, taking in as much of the soothing scent as possible. Nino's cronies had found her. No doubt about it now.

She turned on the faucet and splashed water on her face. No way would she be responsible for anyone else getting hurt. This ended right now. "Okay, Nino, you win," she said to herself in the mirror. "I'll get you what you want."

She unhooked the latch on the small window, lifting the wood frame carefully. Before she climbed through, she checked around for the snowmobile and Blaine, but she didn't see either of them. She stepped onto the toilet and hoisted herself up, lifting herself feet first, then jumped from the window.

The police station was about five miles away. It would take her about an hour to get there, more in the snow. Maybe she should just call Nino and have whoever had just tried to kill her come get her. Save her some time. Then they could just go get what Nino came for and then...

"This is nuts," she whispered.

"You certainly are," Blaine's smooth voice echoed in the night.

She looked around the front yard. She hadn't taken more than ten steps when she'd heard his voice. "Where are you?" she demanded.

"Right here," he whispered in her ear.

"Asshole." She whipped around "I've always hated the way you sneak up on people."

"And I'm not too keen on how you always run out on me." His biceps bulged as he folded his arms across his broad chest. His deadly stare didn't help calm her nerves.

"It's not exactly running out on you this time."

"Then what exactly are you doing out here?"

"You wouldn't understand."

"Probably not," he said as a slight hum in the

distance caused his gaze to shift. "Come on, let's get inside. I feel like an ice cube."

"I can't keep putting your family in danger."

"We've been over this." He tucked her under his arm and started pulling her toward the house.

"If I go back, he'll leave you alone." She cringed at the thought.

"Maybe. But then you'd be dead." His hand shifted down her spine, painfully reminding her of the damage to her back. "I'm a cop. I get paid to put my life on the line to make sure you don't have to."

"But I could leave, and you couldn't stop me, right?"

"I suppose."

"I'm not a suspect anymore, right?"

Sirens flared and flickered as a fire engine and sheriff's car pulled in. Blaine waved at them and then pointed at Dave. "Not technically, but I could arrest you for obstruction of justice." His grip increased. "Don't push me to that. I know there are a few things you're not telling me."

"You don't understand. I can't tell you. I do that, and he'll for sure kill you."

"I understand you're in way over your pretty little head. And if you try to go it alone, I will be investigating your murder. I'm not prepared to do that." He gave her a good shove toward the house. Shima and Emma stood at the front door with their arms crossed, both staring at her.

Kaylee glanced toward the garage. Dave and Toby stood with hoses as dark smoke filled the air.

"Get in the house," Blaine ordered.

"You've got a lot of nerve," Emma said, opening the door. "Don't you get it?"

"I think she does," Shima said quietly, closing the door behind her. "What she doesn't get is we all are here to help her."

"Pretty stupid to go running off into the night when someone just lit the house you're in on fire."

"We don't know she's the target," Shima said, as she poured some hot water into some mugs.

"We all know I'm the target." Kaylee grabbed one of the cups, stirred the dark liquid, and then blew on it.

"Have you told Blaine what's really going on?" Emma asked.

"Some of it," Kaylee admitted.

"Why'd you try to run off?" Emma turned to face her. She really was a pretty woman. Her hair fell to her shoulders, and her light-brown eyes were soft and caring. This Emma Kaylee could like.

"I figured I could walk to the station, get my car, and run off to the guy who's behind all this. Finally putting an end to it," Kaylee said.

Emma shook her head. "You realize how stupid you sound?"

Kaylee nodded. "Yeah. I actually thought about calling Nino and asking him to send his sidekick to come get me and take me to my car."

"More like take you right to the morgue," Emma replied.

Kaylee laughed. It wasn't funny. Not even close. Emma smiled and let out a slight chuckle. It was a nice sound.

"Ladies," Shima said, looking quite shocked. "I don't know who this Nino character is, and I don't understand what is so funny."

"I'm sorry." Kaylee placed her cup down and stood next to Shima. "Nino is a guy I used to work for, and he hired someone to scare me when I found out he worked with the mob and I got my fingers in things I shouldn't have." Kaylee realized she needed to spread some honesty. Trying to leave was beyond stupid. She didn't want to put these people in danger, but since they weren't going to go away, they needed to know a little more of what her situation was.

"What?" Shima dropped the bag of marshmallows on the floor. "You're involved with the mob?"

"I was," Kaylee said. "But not by choice."

"Good God." Shima sat down at the kitchen table.

"Anyway, I thought if I left here, you all would be safe since it's me he wants." And all the stuff I took.

Shima looked up at Kaylee. Her eyes filled with love and concern "But *you* wouldn't be safe, and what the hell good would that do?"

"I know." Kaylee grabbed her mug and sat down. "But no matter where I go, I'm not safe. Nor is anyone who is with me. I hate doing that to all of you."

"I got shot at by a client once," Emma said.

"I got threatened by a student with a loaded gun," Shima added.

"This isn't making me feel better about the situation." Kaylee knew they were trying to tell her everyone's been in danger at some point. "And don't start in with what a crazy man Toby is or how it's Dave and Blaine's job."

"Okay," Shima and Emma said in unison.

"But you have to tell Blaine the whole truth,"

Emma said, patting Kaylee's hand.

"I can't."

"Why not?" Emma asked.

"He'll have to arrest me."

"I think I'll pretend you didn't say that." Shima rubbed her temples.

"Maybe you and I should talk," Emma added. "Alone."

"That might be better." Kaylee rose and leaned against the back door, staring out across the yard. The cold air seeped into the house, giving her the chills. It appeared the flames had been put out and the firemen were pulling out of the driveway.

Toby and Blaine started up the stairs to the apartment as Dave headed toward the main house. He looked worn and tired. She flung the door open for him while he brushed the snow off his coat. "The fire was contained to the car. You girls can go back to Blaine's."

"They didn't find the guy, did they?" Kaylee asked, knowing how good Nino's guys were.

"Toby tracked him and got a plate number. Jonesy's running it now." Dave kicked off his boots. "But for the moment, I think we should all try to get some sleep."

"Are we safe here?" Shima asked.

"I've got Jonesy and a part-timer to hang close. The State Police said they'd up their patrols in this area."

"You girls be careful, okay?" Shima hugged Kaylee and whispered, "Don't run from your problems. They only follow you wherever you go."

Didn't she know it? "You be careful, too."

Emma locked her arm with Kaylee's as they slowly made their way across the yard.

"Can I trust you?" Kaylee asked.

"Yes," Emma said. "Whatever it is you're afraid to tell Blaine, you can tell me. But let's do it another day. You kind of ruined my night with my boyfriend, and I'd like to get back to that."

"You and Toby?" Kaylee shook her head. "You do know what he's like, right?"

"For the last few months, he's been all mine." Emma looked up toward the garage apartment. "Come on, let's go inside."

Kaylee followed Emma up the stairs and into Blaine's apartment where she took off her shoes and hung up her coat. Blaine and Toby both leaned against the kitchen counter, beers in hand and a pile of nachos between them.

"Damn asshole shot at me," Toby said. "I really hate being shot at."

"Glad the asshole missed and hit the snowmobile instead." Emma eased her way over to Toby and tucked herself under his arm. Toby kissed her temple as he pulled her in tight.

Kaylee leaned against the side wall.

"Hit the gas tank, and now we're stranded here for the night. The roads are horrible, so taking Blaine's truck is out of the question. Besides, it's just going to get worse out there." Toby continued to stroke Emma's arm.

Kaylee didn't mean to stare, but when she knew Toby, no girl could get within five feet of him without permission. He didn't date a girl more than once, maybe twice if she was lucky, but never did Toby ever show any public displays of affection.

"You can stop staring," Toby said. "Emma's been drugging me. Only way to make me act like a fool in love."

Emma laughed. "You wish that was your excuse."

"Did you just use the word love?" Kaylee asked.

"Much to everyone's surprise, I am human." He eyed the room. "But I'm more concerned about where I'll be sleeping tonight."

"The couch folds out into a bed," Blaine said.

"That takes care of me and Emma. What about

you and Kaylee?" Toby smiled, as if amused by the situation.

Blaine's face tightened, and he tossed his beer cap on the counter. "She can have my bed."

"I'll take the floor," Kaylee blurted out. She understood why he was mad, her trying to run off again. She couldn't blame him.

Blaine shrugged. "Have it your way." He rinsed his beer mug, tossing it in the sink. "There's a sleeping bag in the closet, along with a small bedroll. Good night."

"Asshole," Emma said.

Blaine stopped halfway up the stairs, but didn't turn when he said, "She can have the bed if she wants. It's her choice."

Kaylee got herself into the bathroom, found her muscle relaxants, and popped two. She forced herself to follow her routine, showering, changing, and brushing her teeth before she re-entered the family room, praying Blaine had remained upstairs.

"We thought you might have made a window," Toby teased.

"I'm not going to try to run again." Kaylee wasn't in any mood to go at it with the 'good-natured-nothing-affects-me' Toby. She grabbed the sleeping bag from the closet and started to roll it out.

"Sleep with Emma on the sofa bed." Toby touched her shoulder. When she looked up at him, she saw a depth inside his eyes she'd never seen before. "Girls can do that shit all the time. I'll take the floor."

"It's okay, Toby, really. I'll be fine." She forced back the tears that threatened to roll down her cheeks. The floor felt hard against her butt when she sat down on the bedroll, but sometimes the hard floor was exactly what her back needed. "So, tell me, how did you two hook up?"

"I hired him to help me investigate a case, and he just wouldn't go away. He was like a stray dog and no matter what I did, he kept showing up."

Toby laughed. "Like I said, she's drugging me."

Kaylee glanced between Toby, who was standing near the kitchen, and Emma, who had climbed onto the pullout. Emma was petite and gorgeous, but in a very reserved way. Toby was rough and big, like a grizzly mountain man. They looked like complete opposites, but when you looked at them, they seemed to fit.

"If you don't mind me asking," Kaylee said. "What's the history between you and Blaine?"

"I don't want to hear this," Toby grumbled something, then got himself a beer and headed for the bathroom.

"It's a pretty simple story. We dated for a while. It didn't go well. He's always been hung up on you, and I got tired of competing with you. He kept saying he was over you, but I doubt he's ever truly gotten past you running."

Kaylee let out a huge puff of air. "We didn't communicate with each other very well, especially after our son died."

"I'm sorry."

"Thanks," Kaylee said. "Seems to be some resentment between you and Blaine. At least that is what I sensed when I first met you."

"I was defending this guy who'd been accused of beating and raping his wife. My job was to give him the best possible defense, and Blaine had been the arresting officer."

"Ouch," Kaylee said, knowing how Blaine felt about domestic violence. "While you were dating Blaine?"

Emma nodded. "The problem was I knew he was guilty, but I was able to get him off on a technicality." Emma glanced at the loft as if she could read Kaylee's mind, wondering if Blaine was listening to the whole conversation. "Anyway, the next day he fatally beat his wife and daughter and then tried to kill himself. It took almost a year and a half to get a final sentencing."

"Has Blaine ever considered blaming the system? Instead of the people who use the system?" Kaylee wondered out loud.

"Actually, he blamed himself because the technicality had been faulty police procedure, but he got ticked at me for using it, and now two innocent people are dead."

"I can see how that would end a relationship."

"Not sure you could call what we had a relationship. It didn't last very long, and it was really over before it started."

"You love Toby?" Kaylee asked.

A broad smile came across Emma's face, and a sparkle filled her light-brown eyes.

"She'd better," Toby said, leaning on the doorjamb. "Otherwise I might have to do something crazy."

"You are crazy." Emma threw back the covers. "Shut the lights off."

Darkness filled the room. Kaylee lay on her back, arms folded on her stomach. The floor wasn't that bad. As long as she didn't move. The wind rustled the tree branches outside. She focused on that until she heard the stairs creak. She tipped her head up to see Blaine coming down the steps.

"Bathroom," he said.

"Shhh."

"Oh, shush yourself," he said, slamming the bathroom door.

"He's in a mood," Emma said.

"Kaylee running out on him tends to piss him off to the point of being an asshole," Toby said.

"You could have said that nicely," Emma said.

"It's all right." Kaylee let out a long breath. "Toby is right. Had I not run off, we all might be sleeping in a bed."

Toby laughed. "Just go up there. He's not going to kick you out."

"True," Kaylee said as she rolled herself to a sitting position just as the bathroom door opened.

Blaine took two steps toward her, bent over, and lifted her into his arms. "One more word from anyone in this room about any sleeping arrangements, and I'll handcuff you for the night."

"Put me down," she said.

"I guess you like handcuffs."

"I didn't say anything about sleeping arrangements. I just told you to put me down."

A few muffled laughs came from the other side of the room as Blaine carried her up the stairs, then gently placed her on the bed.

"Move over."

"What is wrong with you?" she whispered. "Why are you being such a jerk?"

"Because the make-up sex with you is soooo good." He slipped between the covers, pulling her close.

"You do realize that other people can hear you," she whispered.

"Do you think I care?"

"Maybe I care."

"Then stop talking and go to sleep." He tucked her backside up against him and actually let out a sigh.

"I'm sorry," she said. "I'm done running." The lights from the yard filtered through the window. Blaine rolled her to her stomach and lifted the back of her shirt, tracing his fingers across her scars. He kissed her shoulder then cupped her chin, tilting her head upward. "Running from De Luca? Or running in general?"

She sucked in a breath. The implication of his words cut as deep as the scars he was gently rubbing. "You're asking if I'll stay here."

"Yes."

"I don't know," she said.

"If you still want to leave after we figure all this out, I won't stop you."

"There are some things you should know."

"In the morning." He kissed her lips. "Sleep."

9

B laine didn't dare stir. The warm body sprawled out over him brought back memories he'd been trying to forget. But now he wanted to bring them all to the present and make them his future.

He peeked open one eye, thankful the room was still dark. Prying open both eyes, he glanced at the clock. Only five in the morning. He should be good for another hour, so he relaxed and tried to drift back to sleep only to be roused by his cell.

He managed to keep one arm around Kaylee while he snagged the vibrating gadget. Dave's number appeared on the small screen.

"Was that your phone?" she whispered.

"Go back to sleep," he said. "Hello?"

"Sorry to have to wake you," Dave said.

"No problem. What's up?" Blaine wrapped his free arm around Kaylee, nestling her head to his chest. It was like she'd never left ten years ago.

"We need to get out on patrol. Everything is going to be shut down. The other side of the lake is without power, and we're asking for no unnecessary travel."

"Give me five." Blaine flicked on the small reading lamp. "Toby can hang here with the girls and my mom."

"My brother's coming to get Shima to take her to the farm."

Blaine thought about that for a moment. She would be safer at the Whitcomb Horse Farm since most of the help lived on the property, along with Dave's brother and his family.

"I can have everyone transported there," Dave said.

"Actually, I'd like to get Kaylee over to her father's house and have her go through it. Can you take Kaylee, Toby, and Emma to the Mead residence before your brother takes my mom to the farm?"

"Shouldn't be a problem. Now get your ass in gear."

Blaine dropped the cell phone on the nightstand.

"I don't really want to go back to that house right now," Kaylee said.

"I need you to." He ran a hand through his long hair, pushing it from his face. "I've got a theory."

"I think we both agree it's Nino who is behind all this."

"Probably, but I need you to start looking for something specific." Adjusting the covers, he looked at her. Waking with her had been natural, like she should be there with him every night, but at the same time, he knew he had to pull away from her. He had a job to do.

"What?" She sat up, pulling the sheet up to her chin. "What am I looking for?"

"Secret room. Phone records, credit card bills, old letters—anything dated back from about a year before you were born until right after your extended hospital stay when you were six."

"I wouldn't have a clue as to where he kept those things."

"Hadley's looking through old tax returns and anything he has, but he swears he doesn't know who your father could be."

"You don't believe him, do you?"

"I believe he thinks he's doing the right thing by your parents. His loyalty runs deep, but he's also hiding something. I'm afraid he might be putting himself in an awkward position."

"I can relate," she muttered. "I need to tell you something," she said, pushing at his chest.

"Don't tell me, tell Emma. Your lawyer."

"But—"

"No." He kissed her good and hard, making sure she'd be speechless when he came up for air. "Tell Emma and let her deal with it. I'll deal with it after I've figured out who killed your father."

"What about Nin—"

He covered her mouth with his hand. "I suspect all this is highly criminal, which is why I haven't pushed too hard. Best to tell Emma. She can protect you legally. She'll let me know whatever it is I need to know."

"I've so screwed up, haven't I?" she whispered.

"Don't look back, just move forward."

"Easier said than done."

He shifted the covers and swung his legs to the side of the bed. Part of him really wanted to know what she'd done to be in so deep with a man like De Luca, but if he did and it was illegal, he'd be in one hell of a predicament.

"Blaine?" Her voice rang out soft and sweet.

"What, babe?"

"Be careful."

He smiled, remembering his first day of working as a police officer and she'd said those same words. They'd been married for a few months, and she'd gotten up, made him breakfast, and tried like hell not to cry because she was so scared he'd get shot. Back then he had wanted to laugh because not much happened in this sleepy little town, but today...today he didn't want to laugh.

"I will. You promise to hang close to Toby and Emma?"

She slipped her arms around him, pressing her lips against his bare chest. "I'll get up and make you something to eat."

"That will wake Toby and Emma. I'll be just fine."

"You never go five minutes without food."

"I'll figure something out, just go back to sleep." He kissed her temple and tucked her back into bed, hoping the work day wouldn't be too long. He wanted to rummage through that house.

"Do you think that a secret room really exists?" Kaylee asked.

"You lived there, not me." Blaine finished getting dressed.

"My mother said that's how Daddy spied on her. Once she woke me in the middle of the night to go search for the room. She'd been drinking, and I...I...I was terrified I'd turn out just like her."

Blaine looked down at the beautiful vision lying in his bed. "You're not your mother."

She rose up on an elbow. "Thank you."

"For what?"

"For not throwing me to the wolves."

"I wouldn't ever do that." He sighed and then made his way down the dark stairs. Emma and Toby didn't move, so Blaine just slipped on his boots and grabbed his coat and gun. Hopefully the wind would die down, the sun would come out, and the day wouldn't be too long. He wanted in that house. That room was somewhere inside and he knew it.

———

After hours of shoveling cars out of snowbanks, putting groceries away for half the elderly in the community, and finding two missing dogs, Blaine's body begged for a rest, but his mind was still agonizing over Kaylee and her predicament.

"You wouldn't believe all the crap I've found on this De Luca guy," Stacey, the secretary, said. "He's involved in a high-profile murder, and the Grand Jury is discussing the possibility of indicting him and half his family on all sorts of charges."

Blaine took the cup of coffee she offered him and stared into the black liquid like it had all the answers. "Remember, this is unofficial." Unofficial or not, he'd taken an oath, one he was duty-bound to uphold. Right now, he was glad Kaylee hadn't told him much of anything.

"Well, this jelly doughnut isn't unofficial."

"Aw, shucks." He smiled, taking the doughnut. "Best way to a man's heart."

"I don't want your heart, Blaine, just a few answers."

"It's better if you don't ask, that way if I screw up, I won't take you down with me."

"I don't mind bending the rules for you," Stacey said. "But I'd like to know why the sudden interest in the mob." She gave him a pointed look. For a young girl of maybe twenty-three, Stacey was one smart woman.

"I think they might have set my Mustang on fire."

"Why would you think that?" she asked with her

head cocked to the side and both her hands firmly planted on her hips.

He took a long sip of his coffee, ignoring Stacey's glare. She'd been working for the department since she was eighteen, and was a wealth of knowledge, but too damn nosey for her own good. She was also dating a local firefighter, who'd been at his house last night. He was sure she'd gotten all sorts of unofficial information.

"I know that fire was set on purpose, but it wasn't to get at you," she said with a clipped tone.

"Stay out of it, Stacey. Let me do my job."

"Your job doesn't include harboring a material—"

"Stop right there," Blaine said. "Someone shot at a guest of mine, then tried to light my house on fire. My job is to find that person and make sure they suffer the consequences of their actions." He paused to take a deep breath. "It's not my job to interrogate my houseguests when they haven't done anything wrong."

"I don't think you know who you're dealing with." Stacey gave him a level stare. "Here's what I found." She tossed a file onto his desk.

"Thank you."

"You're welcome. Now watch your back." She stormed out of his office.

He'd been bending the rules since he knew how, not to the point of breaking the law, but just enough to keep informed. The more information he had about De Luca, the better. Although, before looking at these files, he needed Emma to pull out any incriminating information on Kaylee.

If it was documented and staring at him in the face, he'd be forced to act. Not something he was prepared to do, and not just because she was sharing his bed again.

Heavy footsteps down the hallway indicated Dave was on his way. Blaine stuffed the files into his backpack and set them aside. Dave was a rules man and didn't always approve of Blaine's methods, but he'd never called him on them as long as Blaine didn't blatantly wave them under Dave's nose. And it didn't cause another "technicality."

"I'll split the night shift with you," Dave plopped himself in the chair, rubbed his scruffy face, and closed his eyes. "We'll go back to regular rotation on Monday, but you and I've got to take tonight and tomorrow night."

"I'll take the second half, both nights."

Dave arched a brow. "You want to trade off around three in the morning?"

"Yeah, but I'm taking Monday off."

"You've already got Monday off this week."

Blaine shook his head. "No, I don't."

Dave grunted something, then rolled his head to the side. "Do I have Monday off?"

"Yep."

"Wonderful. Before I forget, the bullet we dug out of Toby's snowmobile matches the bullets we found in your yard."

Blaine slipped his arms through his coat. "What about the car?"

"Stolen two days ago. The owner reported it immediately, and State filed the report."

"So we're still chasing a ghost."

"I also got an ID on some prints lifted off Rutherford's house."

That stopped Blaine at the door. "Really?" He turned back to look at his boss. "And?"

"Mrs. Linda Hicks. She'd been fingerprinted when she volunteered at the elementary school."

"Interesting," Blaine said. "So I get to ask her a few questions?"

"You can ask her when the last time she saw him was and if she was at the house, but since they were friends at one time, it's possible her prints could be in the house."

"Well, let's find out what she has to say." Blaine turned on his heels and headed out of the station. His first stop would be the burger joint on the way out of town, then he'd pay a little visit to the Hicks' household.

The sun began to dull as it made its descent into the western sky. The snow was piled high, but the air hadn't lost its frigidness, not yet giving way to spring warmth.

Blaine finished his burger and fries in record time and was still hungry when he pulled into the lavish home of Reverend Hicks. He tried to remember everything he could about every encounter he'd had with the Hickses over the years and came to one very simple conclusion. They were too perfect. He couldn't find one thing out of place, except for the odd relationship the good Reverend had with Rutherford.

They'd been friends for years, and to find out Rutherford went back on his word with the Reverend and his church did seem out of the ordinary. As did their friendship. Rutherford wasn't a church-going man. The Catholics would call him a C and E or Christmas and Easter kind of worshiper. Blaine got the distinct impression that Mrs. Hicks didn't really like Rutherford all that much, but she tolerated him.

Blaine looked around the snowy yard and the manicured home. Linda had always been the kind of woman who demanded perfection. Rachael used to say that her mother told her, "You must always look good on the outside, because that is what people will see." Blaine couldn't wait to find out what skeletons lurked in their closets.

He made his way up the snowy porch, rang the doorbell, and waited. He could hear faint voices, but he couldn't make out what they were saying.

"Why, hello, Blaine." Reverend Hicks waved him in as he pushed back the door. "What brings you out here on a snowy day like today?"

"Official business."

A shocked look followed by a nervous smile appeared on Jack's face.

"I'd like to speak with Mrs. Hicks, if you don't mind, sir." Blaine looked around the foyer. The smell of something sweet lingered in the air.

"She's a little under the weather right now."

"What's wrong?" Blaine asked.

"Nothing serious, just a touch of the flu. Maybe you could come back another day."

"You understand I don't like doing this to you, but we have reason to believe she might have seen Rutherford Mead the night he died." Blaine tried to look as sympathetic as possible. "You understand."

Jack nodded. "I saw him the day before."

"You and him had a falling out?" Blaine rested a hand on Jack's shoulder.

"Somewhat. He told me about the change in his will. I wasn't happy about it, but it's his house and she is his daughter. I'm glad he wanted to reconcile with her."

"We know Rutherford couldn't have been Kaylee's biological father." Blaine studied Jack's face, looking for any clue . "Any idea who it could be?"

"Why do you want to know? That's a personal thing and up to Kaylee."

"Not sure, but perhaps it has something to do with Rutherford's death."

"I see," Reverend Hicks said. "I hate to point the finger at anyone, but Hadley Danks would be my guess. However, that would be pure speculation on my part."

"Why Hadley?"

"He was dating her right before Rutherford was."

"How well did you know Roberta?"

"She liked to come to church. She wasn't a happy soul and sought solace in God."

Blaine wondered what else she sought at the church. "Would you mind asking Mrs. Hicks if I could just have a moment of her time and then I'll be on my way?"

"Let him in," a gruff female voice said from the other room.

Blaine was ushered into the family room where the first thing he noticed was the sweet smell had gotten stronger. The second thing was Mrs. Hicks was hiding something under the blanket she'd just thrown around herself.

She coughed. "What do you need, young man?"

"Have you been at the Meads' house in the last few weeks?"

"I have."

"And what were you doing there?" Blaine asked.

"Delivering an antique piece he'd bought from my daughter. I'm working for her part-time now."

"Did you notice anything odd or out of the ordinary?" Blaine scanned the clutter-free room. Not a speck of dust anywhere.

"Rutherford had been acting odd ever since he'd decided to try and get that wayward daughter of his to come home, ungrateful young lady that she is."

"Linda—"

"Well, it's true, but then again, you understand all about that little operator, don't you, Officer Walker?" She hiccupped, and Blaine got a good whiff of alcohol.

Blaine ignored the dig. "Is there anything else you could tell me that might help us find out who killed Rutherford?" Blaine asked, knowing this interview was going nowhere fast. He'd need to do a little digging and come back when he had a better handle on the situation.

"Just that he went back on his word. We could have done so much for the community with that house. We'd planned on turning it into a retreat for our youth, maybe even a summer camp."

"That sounds very nice, Mrs. Hicks. If you think of anything else that might help, don't hesitate to call me. I can see myself out." He held his hand out toward the Reverend who'd been sitting down in a chair near the window, never looking at his wife. The Reverend shook it weakly.

Blaine walked slowly to the front door, admiring the antique furniture and the paintings on the wall.

As he made his way to his car, his mind raced with a million questions.

During the ride to the Mead house, Blaine couldn't remember a time when he'd seen Mrs. Hicks drunk, or even having anything other than a glass of wine here or there. She'd always been prim and proper. She was the walking definition of stuck up.

Rachael had once told him she thought her parents might get a divorce because all they ever did was fight. She mentioned something about her mother being upset that the good Reverend had spent too much time with the problems of other people instead of with his own family. At the time, Blaine had brushed it off because he figured it was the Reverend's job, but maybe Rachael had a point. He flipped open his cell and hit star one, calling his mother.

"Hi, honey," his mother answered. "Mrs. Tillman called and said you helped her grandson find his dog."

"It was one of those days. Where are you?"

"I'm at the farm."

"You planning on spending the night there?" Blaine didn't really want to know, but under the circumstances, he wanted to know his mother would be safe.

"I am," she said.

"All right. I don't know where I'll be tonight, and I just didn't want you to be alone with all that is going on."

"It's been a bit scary."

"Can I ask you something?" Blaine wasn't sure this was the right time or place, except he was relying on Dave to protect his mother.

"Sure."

"Do you love him?"

Blaine pulled into the long, unplowed gravel drive to the Mead residence, hoping his patrol car would make it without getting stuck.

"I do," she said.

"Does he make you happy?" Blaine asked.

"He does."

"Then I'm happy."

"I miss your father," she said softly. "Dave still misses Sally. We have a common bond that brought us together."

"I'm good with it," he said. "And Dad is good with it." He covered his heart, knowing his father was looking down at them, and smiled. His father had always told them that the dead wanted the living to not only continue breathing, but to truly be happy. His mother was doing just that. "I'll talk to you tomorrow."

"Blaine?"

"What?" He rolled the patrol car to a stop behind his pickup and Toby's rusty old Jeep.

"I can feel your confusion. Follow your heart this time."

His heart had lied to him before. "Right now, I'm tracking a killer; my heart has nothing to do with it. Good night, Mother." He flipped off his phone. His heart had everything to do with it, but he couldn't afford to let it get in the way.

10

Kaylee stood alone in her father's room, her heart pounding so fast, sweet beading across her forehead. The room hadn't changed at all since she'd left. The light-brown walls looked freshly painted, but they were the same color. The comforter was still green, and the furniture the same dark cherry her parents had always had. Her father wasn't too keen on change.

She took a deep breath and noticed a faint rosy smell. Wrinkling her nose, she tried to figure out why the aroma was so familiar. Unable to place it, she lifted the bed ruffle, finding a bunch of shoeboxes. She figured they were his old slippers, but she pulled them all out anyway and placed them on the bed.

"Hey," a voice called from behind her.

She jumped, letting out a gasp as she turned. "Emma, you scared me."

"Sorry." Emma glided across the large room, the hardwood floors rattling. She plopped herself down on the edge of the bed. "I can't believe you grew up here. It must have been so cool." She swiped her hand over the lush bedspread.

Kaylee let out a dry laugh and looked at Emma. Kaylee had spent most of the last ten years not letting too many people in. She didn't trust easily, and when she did, it was always the wrong person. Something about Emma made Kaylee feel more comfortable than she was used to.

"Not so much when your mother's schizophrenic and your father's busy making his millions. He didn't even have time for a goodnight kiss most days." Kaylee studied the soft expression on Emma's usually stern face. She could be so professional and unapproachable at times, but when they were just hanging out, she was a completely different person.

"Was it really that bad?" Emma's smile dropped a little.

"I was expected to cover up my mother's illness and many indiscretions. My father demanded that I be the best and be friends with a certain class of people. I was told to be nice and considerate, but dating Blaine sent my father on a rampage. He accused me of using Blaine just to get attention."

"Did you?"

Kaylee narrowed her eyes, though it was an honest question. One she'd answered many times. "I hid my relationship with Blaine for nearly a year until Rachael spilled the beans."

"Toby really doesn't like her much."

"She's not so bad. And Toby can be a judgmental dick who knows how to hold a grudge." Kaylee opened the first box with trembling fingers, glad Emma was in the room, just in case she found something unnerving. "My father had way too many slippers." She examined the expensive suede custom-made slippers before putting them back in the box.

"Is Rachael a good friend of yours?"

"We were best friends in high school, but when I went to Europe after I lost my son, she thought I was nuts. We got in a huge fight, and until the other day, I hadn't spoken to her in years. She can be misguided and seriously way too self-centered, but I've missed her over the years. Her heart is in the right place." Kaylee sat on the bed next Emma.

"You're very beautiful when you're not acting like a total bitch."

Emma laughed. "Toby says I look like an uptight *fucking* bitch when I'm working."

"No offense, but I thought you were an ice princess."

Emma's smile illuminated the room when she laughed. "When I presented my first case, I came into court all warm and bubbly. No one took me seriously. My boss kept trying to tell me to act tougher—be ruthless—but I didn't get it. Then the judge told me if I was going to be successful, I needed to learn to leave the niceness at the door."

That explained the Gemini personality. "I guess you took their advice," she paused and then said, "I didn't want to like you."

"Yeah, well, that feeling was mutual."

Kaylee laughed. "I have no right to be jealous; I'm the one who left and filed for divorce."

"You're an only child?" Emma asked, taking Kaylee's hand in hers.

The closeness Emma offered made Kaylee uncomfortable, and she slid her hand away. "I've always wished I had a sister."

"I have an older sister. When we were young, I

hated her, but now we're very close. She lives in St. Paul, so I don't get to see her much."

Kaylee's breath hitched. It had been a long time since she had a friend she could just sit and hang out with. It felt good and that scared Kaylee. "Any other siblings?"

"A younger brother who works on Dave's farm. He's still trying to find himself or some such nonsense. My parents live in Grand Forks, and they love Toby. Go figure."

"So do you." Kaylee smiled. "I never thought I'd see the day Toby would fall in love."

"From what I hear, he never lasted more than two nights with a woman. That made him more appealing."

Kaylee lifted a brow.

"No other woman for me to live up to."

"Blaine got over me years ago."

"You know that's not true. Hell, he scooped you up last night and carried you off to his bed. Kind of romantic."

"He felt guilty because of these." Kaylee lifted her T-shirt to show her scars. "Nino De Luca hired someone to do this to me." Kaylee heard a gasp escape Emma's lips, and she yanked her shirt down in shame. "He'll stop at nothing to make sure I don't tell the truth, so Romano will walk."

"Sam Romano? But they just arrested him. I've heard the D.A. in Chicago is trying to get a bunch of people who work for De…holy shit."

"You got it. Before I got stabbed, I'd been collecting information on a different case I thought was being mishandled. They were setting up an innocent man so their guy would walk. I even talked with an FBI agent."

"What did you do with the things you were collecting?" Emma's eyes were wide.

"I hid them in my apartment, but the asshole who stabbed me found them and gave them to Nino."

"Why'd you go back?"

"No one believed me, or at least I didn't think anyone would. I didn't think I had a choice. Nino paid for my hospital stay and all my physical therapy. He also threatened me on a daily basis. I was scared, but I wanted out."

"Jesus." Emma took Kaylee by the hand. "I greatly misjudged you."

"Why do you say that?"

"You're a very brave woman to go up against those guys."

"Brave?" Kaylee said dryly. "Scared shitless is more like it. I went back because I didn't want to die. Then in order for me 'live,' I had to take my old job back, and I had to testify on Sam's behalf, becoming his alibi. So I did."

"Did you give a sworn statement?"

"Yes."

"Whoa, wait. Do you know for sure Sam murdered those guys?"

"No, but I wasn't with him at the times I said I was. I left a note for the FBI guy who had been hounding me to flip. He said he could protect me, but at the time, I didn't think anyone could. I thought if I got enough money, I could leave the country. Hence the trip back here. Before I left, I sent the FBI agent some materials I stole from Niño's office that are incriminating, and I took off."

Emma shook her head, then said, "Does Blaine know any of this?"

"No."

"Thank God. If he knew, he'd have to call the FBI, and they'd get a federal marshal over here and haul your ass back to Chicago. Did you know Niño tried to report you missing?" Emma rolled her hair into a ponytail, and her face turned serious.

"Why would he do that?"

"If the cops find you first, he'll say you took stuff. He'll claim you stole it and doctored it. I wouldn't be surprised if he has a laundry list of things you did. But, if he finds you first…"

Kaylee's body trembled from the inside out. "How do you know so much about all this?"

"I'm a criminal lawyer. I'm always interested in high-profile cases, and I have a morbid curiosity for the mob, being Italian and all."

"I'm in pretty deep, huh?"

Emma nodded. "Does this FBI agent know you left him this stuff?"

"I don't know…probably."

"Oh, Kaylee, you're going to have to go back at some point."

"Like hell." Kaylee had believed she could run off into the night and disappear. She wasn't all that important so they'd forget about her. "I can't go back. You don't know what kind of man Nino is."

"I don't mean back to him." Emma stood. "You have to testify. We're going to have to call that agent…soon."

"You're totally insane. Nino will kill me."

"You've got a better chance if you turn on him. Come on. I'm on your side."

"You saw the scars on my back," Kaylee said.

She hadn't thought about turning against him, just running from him and making sure she stayed alive. "That was only my first warning. I don't think I'll get a second."

"Look." Emma took Kaylee's hands again. "I can help you with the FBI, get them to offer you a deal for your testimony. I can make sure no charges are brought against you for lying and protect you. They do this shit all the time."

"What about Blaine?"

"We have to keep this from him for now, at least until I get a chance to call the feds and figure out our next move."

"Why should I trust you?" Kaylee stood and paced at the edge of the bed. It felt good to get some of this off her chest. She'd been carrying such a heavy load, but by unleashing it meant she had to trust.

"Because I'm all you've got," she said. "And I'm very good at what I do."

Kaylee nodded in acceptance. Working with Emma was better than trying to take off and hide, waiting for someone to kill her.

"I need to do some digging. I've got some contacts in Chicago, but understand that this will be happening pretty quickly once I call that agent."

Kaylee plunked down on the bed again. "I've really screwed up."

"Get over it," Emma said. "You have the opportunity to right a bunch of wrongs, and I'm going to hold you to it."

Kaylee felt safe with Emma and trusted her. "I hid some files in my father's safe," Kaylee said. "Along with the agent's business card."

"You've got to be kidding me." Emma yanked Kaylee by the arm. "You told Blaine you didn't touch anything else in the house."

"I didn't want anyone to know I had this stuff. Every time Blaine caught me running, I was going for the files."

"And then to get the hell out of Dodge."

"I was scared. Blaine thought I killed my father. I was being interrogated—"

"Yeah, I get it." Emma tugged at her arm. "Let's go get the files before Blaine gets back. Can you keep this from him?"

"I have so far."

Kaylee had always been afraid of basements in any house, but her childhood basement just seemed like a creepy movie. The cemented walls had weird water stains that in the dark would come alive. Heck, they came alive when the basement was all lit up.

"Why are we doing this?" she asked Blaine, staring at the grungy walls. The musty smell overpowered her, and she sneezed.

"Because if there is a secret room, I'd bet my paycheck it would be down here."

She continued to knock on the walls, trying to hear something that sounded different from her last knock. At least that's what Blaine said to listen for. "This is nuts."

"'Nuts' would be doing nothing." He took out the tape measure and then bent over, pulling it across the floor. His hair fell in his face, getting in his eyes. He kept flipping his head or using his hand to brush it from his beautiful face.

"Oh, for the love of God," she said, unable to take it anymore. "Here." She took the ponytail holder out of her hair and started to gather up his. "If I didn't love your hair so much, I'd tell you to chop it all off."

"You like my hair?" He winked.

"It's so 'Indian' like." She shoved him in the shoulder and went back to knocking on the wall.

"Wanna be my squaw?"

"Savage." Unable to resist the familiar banter, she looked over her shoulder and smiled.

The smoldering look he cast her as he closed the gap between them should have frightened her, but all it did was ignite the passion deep within her. His powerful body backed her against the wall, and his fierce, steaming eyes made her shiver.

His tongue rolled across his lips as he dipped his head closer. A strong thigh shoved her legs apart as he pushed against her core. Immediate heat poured from her body. It baffled her how one man could make her feel so much, so quickly, allowing her to forget everything else.

There was no denying the passion he invoked in her, and no stopping it either. She slipped her hands under his shirt, feeling the muscles in his back tighten. The warmth of his lips, then the probing of his soft, but demanding tongue made her legs feel like rubber.

"Yo, Dark Man, get up here," Toby called from somewhere above them.

"Busy right now." Blaine cupped her face, his breathing haggard.

"You're gonna want to see this; sucking face can wait."

"He's always had shitty timing," Blaine muttered. "Be right up."

"What are we doing?" she whispered.

He pulled her to his chest and kissed her tenderly. "Saving your ass."

"I don't want to hurt you."

He closed his eyes. "When it's time for you to take care of other things, you can walk away from me if you still want to."

"I won't have a choice."

"We always have choices, but I guess you haven't learned that yet." A slow smile appeared across his face. "Trust me," he whispered, leaning in to kiss her cheek. "And don't deny yourself simple pleasures." He patted her bottom and then pushed her toward the stairs.

"What'd you find?" Blaine said as they approached the top of the stairs.

"We might want to get Dave here." Emma pointed to a spot in the hallway where a picture used to hang. "Did you know about that safe?"

Kaylee shook her head, confused. She thought she knew everything about this house. She thought everyone was nuts for thinking there was a secret room. Nothing secret in this house but who her biological father was. "I knew about the one in the bedroom and the one in Dad's den. This one must be new."

Blaine flipped open his phone and walked away, barking out some orders to whoever answered.

Kaylee took a small step toward the painting that leaned against the wall on the floor just below the safe, one of her father's favorites. "When we spoke right before he died, he told me he had some news for me. News that would be tough to take."

"You think he knew who your father was?" Emma asked, standing next to her.

"I don't know. He never wanted me to ever find that out. At least that is what he told me after Deslin died."

"Why?" Emma asked, as Blaine motioned everyone to the kitchen.

"Because he didn't want another scandal. He didn't want people to talk even more than they already were. It was as if we acknowledged my paternity, it would negate the fact that he'd raised me."

Blaine pulled out a chair, then turned it and straddled it. "Sit," he ordered to the rest of the room. "We'll wait for Dave."

"What crawled up your ass?" Toby asked.

"Sorry," he said. "I'm just tired."

"You have to have some thought about who your father might be," Emma said.

"I didn't even know he wasn't my father until we...until..."

"Until our son had died." Blaine took her hand and laced his fingers through hers.

"It's hard to look at any man my parents' age in this town and wonder if my eyes look like his. Or if I have one of his traits. That's part of why I left." Kaylee turned and faced Blaine. "I never lied to you," she whispered.

"But you didn't talk to me either," he said.

"That cuts both ways," Kaylee said. "My dad wasn't approving of anything I did that wasn't his decision. His plan. So when we lost Deslin, he...he made it even harder on me, and I was so utterly broken by the things he said..."

"I know," Blaine squeezed her hand. "He could be downright mean."

"My father didn't think I could manage on my own. He sent me to Europe. Then he wanted to set me up at his firm because he didn't think I was capable." And the reality of her unsuccessful attempt to have a life of her own came crashing down. She looked deep into Blaine's eyes. "You'd left, and your mother didn't think you were ever coming back. So, I set out to prove my father was wrong about me."

"He was wrong about you," Blaine said. "But I want to know one thing."

"What's that?" Kaylee asked.

"I saw the newspaper clipping of your engagement."

Kaylee laughed. "When I met Nino, I was a cocktail waitress. He came in all the time, asked to sit at my table. Tipped well. But I was struggling to make it on my own. He offered me a job. I took it. He was nice. Sent me flowers. Treated me like a queen until I said yes to marrying him. Then I found out who he really was, but it was too late."

"Did you love him?" Blaine asked.

She shook her head. "He played me. Hit my weak spots. I knew from the start he wasn't the man for me, I just wanted to prove my father wrong. Childish and stupid, I know."

"Not really," Blaine said. "Your father set you up to fail. I know you miss him, and I'm sorry he's gone, but he, whether it be consciously or subconsciously, sabotaged everything you did."

"I don't think it was failure he set up, but he wanted to put me in a bubble, like he tried with my mother. It backfired."

Blaine's chair scratched across the floor as he pushed it and stood. "I think Dave's here," he said.

Kaylee watched Blaine close the door with a gentle tug instead of slamming it like she sensed he really wanted to do. Her father had always been a hot button with him. Her dad had treated Blaine's father like a subpar human being. When Kaylee got pregnant, her father essentially disowned her, unless she had an abortion. That wasn't going to happen, so he pushed her out of his life, thinking she'd come running back.

Out the window, she could see Dave's pickup roll down the long drive.

"You okay?" Emma asked after Toby had gotten up and left the room.

"I am," Kaylee said.

"You're not the warm and fuzzy type, are you?" Emma asked with open arms. "My family's extremely affectionate. I can't walk into my parents' home without a big hug and kiss."

"My parents didn't understand the meaning of human contact. That was really hard for me when Blaine and I first married, but I got used to it until…I think I'd like a hug." Kaylee walked into Emma's arms. It was an uncomfortable feeling at first, but Kaylee could get used to it.

"Aww, can I join in? Better yet, can I take pictures?" Toby teased as he waltzed back into the kitchen.

"Never going to happen, so you can just forget it," Emma said.

"You two naked? Together? Or me watching?"

"Oh...my...God. How the hell did I ever end up in love with an idiot like you?"

"I'm easy to love; it's the loving back part that's got me all confused." Toby's smile was as warm as the affection and love he had in his eyes.

He circled his arms around them both, whispering to Kaylee, "After he finds out who did this, and you take care of your little problem, give him—and yourself—the chance to heal and find each other again." Toby gave Emma a kiss on the temple, then turned and met Blaine and Dave by the door.

Kaylee wanted nothing more than to be in Blaine's arms again, forever, but she couldn't even think about it. Not yet, anyway.

"Kaylee," Dave said, slipping out of his wet coat. "Do you have any problem with us searching this house?"

Kaylee glanced at Emma, who nodded. "Do what you need to."

"You realize anything we find, incriminating or otherwise, could be taken in as evidence," Dave added.

"I understand."

The house phone rang.

"Should I answer it?" She didn't feel like this was her home anymore and didn't know who would be calling her anyway.

"Answer it," Blaine said.

Kaylee picked up the receiver. "Hello?"

"Darlin', I've been looking for you," the voice on the other end of the phone echoed in her ears.

She gripped the receiver and swallowed. Her heart pounded frantically against her ribs, and when she opened her mouth, she couldn't form any words.

Nino had found her.

"Come now, sweetheart, I can hear you breathing."

Kaylee glanced down; Emma had taken her hand as if she knew who was on the other end of the line.

"Who is it?" Blaine whispered.

"What do you want, Nino?" Kaylee asked.

Blaine kept her gaze, mouthing her to keep him on the line. Not something she wanted to do.

"I just want you to come home where you belong."

"We're through, Nino. You don't love me; you've made that painfully clear."

Dave had flipped open his cell while Blaine continued to hold her gaze, giving her strength and comfort.

"Oh, but I do love you, and you must come home. Please don't make me have someone come find you."

"Are you threatening me?"

"Oh, baby, not at all. You see, there is this matter of a criminal case and those documents you stole. I don't want to have to subpoena you. Or worse...have you arrested. You are an important witness, and you must come and testify."

"No, Nino, I won't lie for you."

"Don't be foolish. You know what could happen."

A sudden, sharp twist in her muscle reminded her of what could happen. She could feel herself begin to weaken, but she knew if she caved this time, she'd be dead as soon as she put the receiver down. "I'm not frightened of you anymore."

"Your ex-husband can't help you. As a matter of fact, I could take him out right now."

"Blaine!" she shouted. "He can see you!"

Everyone in the room rushed to her side as she buckled to the ground. "Nino, please don't do this," she whispered, but all Nino did was laugh as the phone went dead.

Strong arms cradled her, lifting her off the floor. "Give her some room," she heard Blaine say.

"He can see us. He said he'd take you out." She looped her arms around his shoulders, burying her face in his neck. "He's going to kill us."

"If he wanted us dead now, I think there'd be gunfire," Toby said.

Blaine carried her into the den. He set her down on the love seat, then sat next to her, drawing her close to his body. She tried to relax, but her body shook. She knew Nino had found her when someone shot at her, but hearing his voice. Hearing his threats...knowing he could make them come true.

"I'm sorry," she whispered.

"It's not your fault."

"I have to take responsibility for my own actions," she said. "Not doing that destroyed us years ago. I'm not going to let it kill us now."

He tilted her chin then brushed his lips against

hers tenderly. "I'm not going to let anyone hurt us anymore."

She wanted to believe that, but life had taught her differently. He kissed her again. His touch was gentle and loving. She clutched at his shoulders, not wanting to let go, but he pushed her back. "As much as I like where this is headed, I have a safe to blow up."

"You're going to do what?"

11

Kaylee swallowed, crossing her arms around her middle.

"Are you sure you want to do this now?" Dave asked.

Kaylee felt the blood drain from her face. "No. I'm not sure, and I'm not the one making some kind of bomb."

"We can open the safe another time," Dave said with soft, caring eyes.

"I think now is good," Blaine said, not looking up from his tools that would safely blow up the safe, at least according to him. Kaylee had to wonder. "I don't want a locksmith coming. I don't want anyone else in this house."

"I don't like bending—"

Blaine interrupted Dave. "You didn't have a problem with it when I suggested it."

"Kaylee," Dave said. "I really need a verbal consent that you want him to do this."

"Just open the damn thing." She wrinkled her nose. "That stuff smells."

Blaine glanced up, his eyes sparkling like a kid in a candy store. Kaylee got the distinct feeling he enjoyed doing this. "You get used to it."

She rubbed her nose. "Not."

"I thought they taught you how to diffuse them, not make them." Dave laced his fingers around Kaylee's forearm. "Maybe we should take a step back." Dave tugged her down the hallway and into the foyer.

Blaine fiddled with some wires and then stepped back with a smile. "If I can't build one, I can't take one apart. If I can't take them apart without blowing myself up, I should have gone into a different line of work." He winked. "Watch this."

A loud pop filled the room as the door to the safe flew from the wall, crashing into the other wall before landing on the floor with a thud.

"Oops. I guess I used too much." Blaine wiped off some of the soot that had reared up and landed on him.

"Glad I stuck with homicide in my early days," Dave muttered.

"You have to be homicidal to work bomb squad," Blaine said.

Kaylee shivered "I can't believe you did shit like that for a living."

"And survived," Toby added, rubbing his scruffy face. "Man, I'm impressed."

"Kaylee, why don't you take a look inside," Dave instructed.

She took small, tentative steps toward the hole in the wall and stood next to Blaine. "Can you see anything?" she asked.

"Just a shoe box." He gave her a reassuring smile, but it didn't really help.

"I can't do this." Kaylee froze.

"Can I look?" Blaine reached into the safe, pulling out a box.

Kaylee just nodded.

"Well?" Dave said.

"Pictures," Blaine said, not looking up, but flipping through them.

"Of what?" Dave asked.

"I think I'll leave the room," Kaylee said, but Dave kept a strong arm on her, foiling her escape.

"What do we know about Rachael and this

boyfriend of hers?" Blaine asked, shifting things around in the box.

"Rachael?" Kaylee ran her trembling fingers across her throat. "What does she have to do with this?"

"Not sure." Blaine tilted his head, showing his dark, intense eyes.

"She told me she thinks he's the one," Kaylee added. "But why do you ask?"

"Poor, unsuspecting bastard, someone should warn him about that wacko," Toby said.

"She's not a wacko," Kaylee argued.

"Wanna bet? She had the balls to claim I was the father of a baby who didn't even exist."

"Why would she do that?" Kaylee knew Toby and Rachael had problems with each other over the years, but this was news to her. "She doesn't even like you."

"All that woman wants is to get married and have a kid," Toby said. "And she doesn't give a damn who it's with. Or who it hurts."

"You and Rachael?" Kaylee asked, staring at Toby.

"Eons ago," he said. "One night."

"Let's focus on Rachael's present love life," Blaine said.

"What do Rachael and her love life have to do with what is in that box?" Dave asked.

"By the looks of these pictures, I think Rachael had an affair with Rutherford."

"Oh, God, no." Kaylee rushed forward and yanked the pictures from Blaine's hands. There had to be some mistake. "Holy shit! Oh, Daddy, what the hell were you thinking?"

Blaine held up a note. "And it looks like she was blackmailing him."

Kaylee knelt next to Blaine. "Why would she do that? She was my friend, why the hell would she sleep with my father? Why would my father sleep with her?" She rocked back on her heels, staring at pictures she wished she'd never seen.

"Kaylee," Dave said as he knelt down beside her and glanced at the photos in her hands. "I need to take these pictures, okay?"

She nodded. "Next thing, you'll tell me the nice police chief here is my dad."

"Impossible...and not funny," Dave said, lifting a brow.

"I'm sorry, but my life has become a comic strip. I need a drink."

"Sounds good to me." Blaine took her by the hand and led her into the family room. Getting good and drunk wouldn't solve anything, but it would take the edge off. She stood in front of her father's liquor stash. She wasn't much of a liquor drinker. She preferred wine, and could tolerate beer, but hard liquor made her sick.

"I'll get you something." He motioned to her father's favorite wingback chair. She settled into the oversized chair. It had been her father's throne, and no one ever sat in it without permission. She watched as Blaine poured two drinks. She'd always liked watching him. He didn't have to be doing anything. Could be reading a book. Sleeping. Whatever. Watching him always made her feel calm. He handed her a drink. She swirled the brown liquid then took a good gulp.

"Whoa." She shook her head. "Just what the doctor ordered."

"What is it about Rachael that appeals to you?" Blaine asked. "I mean, she was always trying to outdo you. Be better than you. Hell, she even made a pass at me while we were together."

"I don't know," Kaylee said. "We've been friends since we could talk."

"But she always tried to put you down."

Kaylee took another long, slow sip. This time it didn't burn as much, but her stomach did sour, sending a warm chill across her middle. "Not really."

"She tried to break us up." He leaned against the bookcase, legs crossed at the ankles in that sexy stance of his.

"So did your parents, my parents, and half this damn town."

"Point taken, but I still don't understand."

"It's not any different than you and Toby."

"Toby has never done anything hurtful to me."

"Maybe not, but he did tell you we were making a mistake by getting married." She tossed back the rest of her drink and then let out a little belch. "Sorry."

"That's different."

She laughed. "He might have been nice about it, but he made his point loud and clear."

"He still stood up with us. He was still there for us. For me."

Blaine was making this too easy for her. She'd be able to make her point and then go pass out. "You had to guilt him into it. He only stood there because he owed you. You two are like brothers. You love him because you don't know anything else, no matter what. I feel the same way about Rachael. She may have done and said some things because she was hurt, or out of spite, but she was always there for me."

"That close friend of yours had an affair with your father," his words were clipped. "Giving her motive to kill him."

Blaine refilled her glass, ignoring his inner conscience. She never could handle her alcohol, but the day's events had been overwhelming. He also understood her point, but it didn't help. Ultimately, it didn't matter. Rachael was now a suspect. "I'll be right back." Blaine handed her the glass and slipped out into the hallway.

"Who takes pictures like this?" Dave asked, going through the box.

"Emma, would you go sit with Kaylee?" Blaine asked. He no longer thought she'd run. He just didn't want her to be alone.

"Sure." Emma squeezed his shoulder and disappeared into the other room.

"These are killing my eyes. I just don't get it. Does everyone take naked pictures these days? Have sex tapes?" Dave dropped the pictures in a bag.

"No, Dad. Only people who want to jerk off… or someone with an agenda," Toby sat down on the steps and rubbed his scruffy beard. "I bet Rutherford didn't even know the pictures existed until she showed them to him."

"Why would he sleep with her? Hell, she's a child." Dave shook his head.

"Am I a child?" Toby asked with a lifted brow.

"You know what I mean. It would be like me going after Emma or Kaylee."

"Not even close, Dad."

"I beg to differ." Dave sat down on the step next to his son. "Rachael had been his daughter's best friend. He's known her since she was in diapers. That's gross."

"But she is—and was—a grown woman in these pictures, and age doesn't necessarily matter in affairs of the heart," Toby said.

Blaine let out a dry chuckle. "Because you're an expert on this subject?"

"No," Toby said. "Just saying."

"How long have you and Emma been seeing each other?" Dave asked.

"About six months," Toby said. "And this has nothing to do with Rachael or Rutherford."

Blaine watched shock register on Dave's face.

Dave had never thought his son would change his wild ways. Hell, neither did Blaine, but sometimes the right woman changed them for you.

"You have a girlfriend," Dave said. "A real girlfriend. I think your mother is dancing in heaven."

"Speaking of Mom," Toby said. "I'd like Emma to be the only one. As a matter of fact, I was hoping to give her Mom's ring."

Blaine slapped his hands together and laughed out loud. He wasn't laughing because it was funny, but the look on Dave's face was classic. "Dave, you okay?"

"Ring? Diamond?" Dave managed between coughs. "You? Emma? Oh, boy. I'd better sit down."

"You are sitting down, Dad." Toby slapped his hand on his father's shoulder.

"Does Emma know any of this?" Blaine asked.

"No, and you better not ruin it," Toby said.

"When are you going to pop the question?" Dave asked.

Toby rubbed his scruffy beard, and his face turned white. "As soon as I get up the nerve."

"That could take a while," Blaine teased. "I could tell her for you."

"You screw this up for me, I'll deck you." Toby stood, eyeing the other room. "You let me handle my love life, okay?" Toby nailed Blaine in the chest with his finger. "You take care of Kaylee."

"Sounds like a plan." Blaine's arms flew wide.

Toby cleared his throat just as Emma appeared in the foyer.

"How's Kaylee?" Dave asked.

"Halfway to drunk, and she's totally creeped out by Rachael and her father. Not to mention the phone call from De Luca." Emma slipped under Toby's arm. "I wouldn't want to be her right now."

"Emma, I'd like a word with you about Kaylee's situation," Dave said.

"Nothing to talk about. She's my client, and I'll make sure things go through the proper channels and your office is covered." Emma smiled. "Blaine, you should go back in there. She's kind of all over the place, and I think she'd rather have you around right now."

"Thanks." Blaine took a deep breath and then peered into the family room.

Kaylee sat right where he'd left her. She'd just emptied another glass. Time to get her to bed.

Blaine helped Kaylee up the stairs and tucked her between the sheets in her father's room. The paleness of her already porcelain skin appeared ghost-like in the dim light. "I'll have Emma make you some French toast and cocoa."

"I'm sorry." She hiccupped, snuggling with the pillow. "I hate to cause you such problems."

"You're not the problem." He forced himself to remain standing, when he really wanted to climb between those covers and hold her.

Her eyelids fluttered open. "Do you really think Rachael could've had an affair with my father?"

"They were having an affair," Blaine said, recalling seeing them at the local diner a few times.

"Not that I don't think my father was attractive, but why would she be interested in him?"

"That's what I intend to find out."

"What about Nino?" She closed her eyes and began to roll away.

"You let me and Emma worry about him." He took a step away from the bed. Deep down he knew in a day or two he'd be forced to turn her over to someone else, or turn his back on everything he believed in.

"Go to sleep," he whispered. He turned off the light and headed down to find Dave. It was time to find out what the hell Rachael was up to.

"You ready?" Blaine asked, grabbing his keys from the counter.

"Any idea where she is?" Dave asked.

"Let's try her house first."

"I'll follow you." Dave opened the door and headed for his pickup.

Once on the road, Blaine radioed the dispatcher to call Rachael.

"Go ahead, she's on the line."

"Ms. Hicks, this is Assistant Police Chief Walker…"

"Why the formalities?" Rachael asked.

"This is official. I need to speak with you."

"Oh my God!" she screeched. "Are my parents okay?"

"They're fine; just sit tight. I'll be there in about ten minutes."

"Okay," she said, and the line went dead.

Thank God. He couldn't handle talking to her another minute. He'd always tolerated her because of Kaylee, but he didn't trust her.

A few gray clouds filtered though the dark sky as evening gave way to night. The air was still crisp and cool, but the softness in the wind gave the subtle hint that old man winter was on his last gasp.

The driveway to Rachael's small, quaint home

was completely cleared of snow, but mounds of the white stuff lined the drive. Blaine wondered how she afforded this house. She'd bought it at the same time she'd started her new antique business, and after she'd done nothing but hop from decorating job to decorating job, not doing much of anything. Blaine wondered who could have been paying her bills when he peeked into her garage to see her shiny convertible and a new Lexus SUV.

Dave knocked on the door, tucking the shoebox under his arm. "Don't get her all defensive."

"Yes, boss."

"I mean it, Blaine." Dave lifted a brow just as the door rattled.

"Good evening." Rachael gave them a half-smile, opening the door and waving them in. "Can I get you something to drink?"

"No, thanks, ma'am," Dave said.

Blaine followed them into the family room, all the while checking out the expensive antique furnishings and paintings. He suspected it had cost a small fortune to decorate this house. "How long have you lived here?"

"I've lived in this town my whole life, except for the four years I was at school."

Blaine wanted to say "no shit," but instead he said, "I meant in this house."

"I bought it about two years ago. It's taken me that long to furnish it." She smiled proudly, offering them a seat.

"It's very nice," Dave said dryly. "I saw a piece like this in Mr. Mead's house."

"Ruth...Mr. Mead did purchase a few items from me recently." Rachael sat down and fiddled with her fingers in her lap.

"Do you have a delivery company?" Blaine asked.

"Many customers pick up their own pieces, but I can deliver. I either do it myself or hire a trucking company. Why do you ask? Do you see something you like? Everything in here is in my shop."

Blaine wanted to laugh out loud, but chose not to. "Did you deliver Mr. Mead's pieces?" Rutherford had been notorious for not liking change, which included new cars, new help, and even new furniture.

Rachael's forced smile turned to a frown. "I'd have to look at my records, and those are at the shop."

"You don't remember?" Dave asked.

"I wouldn't want to give you inaccurate

information. I do know he purchased more than one piece, and at different times."

"I would think you would remember delivering something to an old friend's father or having someone else do it," Blaine added.

"You know, you could be right." Her fake smile returned, and she tapped her finger on her forehead. "My mother might have helped me with one, but the other pieces were pretty large and wouldn't have fit in my truck. I'm sure it was delivered, but I'd have to check. May I ask what this is all about?"

"What kind of relationship did you have with Mr. Mead?" Blaine asked, watching the blood drain from her face.

"He's one of my father's best friends, you know that."

"'We want to know about *your* relationship with him," Blaine said.

"I didn't have a relationship with Mr. Mead."

Dave lifted the top of the shoebox and held up a plastic bag. "These pictures indicate otherwise."

"Oh, my...where did you get those?" Rachael's soft and helpful demeanor was replaced by fear. "Those are personal, and none of your business."

"When a man is murdered, his personal life and

those around him become my business," Dave said, dropping the pictures back in the box. "We found a note indicating that you might use these pictures against him."

"Oh, Christ." Rachael stood and began to pace. "Those pictures were taken while I was in college, and well, the note...let's just say I was young and stupid."

"What do you have to hold over his head?" Blaine asked.

"That I was a young, impressionable girl and my father wouldn't have approved. It would've destroyed their friendship."

"Is that why their relationship was strained?" Something didn't fit, so Blaine took the bag and opened it to get a better look at the pictures.

"Hey!" she shouted. "Do you mind?"

Blaine ignored her and put a couple of pictures together. "How long did the affair go on?"

"Not long."

"From when to when?" Dave asked.

"Started the summer after my freshman year and ended that Christmas."

"You're lying." Blaine showed Dave a couple of pictures.

"How dare you." She reached for the pictures. "Who the hell do you think you are?"

"A cop who needs answers in a murder investigation," Blaine said. "We can do it here or we can take you to the station."

"For what? Sleeping with an older man?"

"For questioning, regarding Rutherford Mead's death," Dave said.

"You think I killed Rutherford? Oh, please."

"Were you having an affair with him when he died?" Blaine asked, holding up what he believed to be a more recent picture.

"No." She gave him a level stare, then plopped back down in the chair. "I wasn't lying when I said it was short-lived while I was in college, but when he loaned me the money to start my business, well…we kind of started seeing each other again. There. Are you happy? This is going to kill Kaylee."

Blaine ignored the comment and continued. "Do you owe him money now?"

"Not really." She stared at Blaine. "He loaned me the money without a contract. I've been paying him back here and there and with some new furnishings. He was the one holding those pictures over my head."

"Why?" Blaine held the pictures up. "To keep you or threaten you?"

"Both," she sighed. "He'd threatened to tell my father if I didn't keep sharing his bed. It wasn't what I wanted."

"What did you want?" Dave asked.

"I want a family…he didn't. I ended the affair, and he'd constantly try to get me to come back by threatening me."

Blaine rubbed his face. "So you decided to take matters into your own hands?"

"I didn't kill him," she said. "I told my parents about us, and they sort of flipped out on me and then on Rutherford." Rachael's eyes darted to the floor. "And that's why Rutherford took my parents out of the will."

"You realize you're not helping your parents much right now." Dave tucked the pictures back into the box.

"My father couldn't hurt a fly, and my mother just thinks Rutherford's a dirty old man." Rachael ran her hands through her hair.

"Years ago, you claimed to know who Kaylee's biological father was," Blaine said.

"Could be half the men in this town. If she

wasn't so blonde, it could have been your father."
She stared at Blaine. "But I had only heard a
rumor."

"And?" Blaine glared at her.

"My mom said Mr. Danks had it bad for Mrs.
Mead in high school, and he blamed Rutherford for
her illness."

"What about your father?" Blaine asked.

"Give it up, Blaine. My father would never
cheat on his wife, much less turn his back on God
like that, especially with a woman as sick as Mrs.
Mead."

"Do you plan on leaving town any time soon?"
Blaine asked, tired of rumors and speculation. He
needed facts, and fast.

"I'm a suspect?"

"Just don't leave town without checking with
us." Dave added and headed toward the door.
"Thanks for your time."

Blaine followed Dave to his patrol car. "You
thinking the same thing I am?"

"That Rachael's hiding something or protecting
someone." Dave nodded. "Go get some sleep. We'll
pay a visit to the Reverend and Mrs. Hicks tomorrow
at church." Dave disappeared into his truck.

The streets were dark, but the large snowbanks glowed in the moonlight. The drive up the gravel road to the Mead house reminded him of the night he'd parked his motorcycle down by the gate and met Kaylee by the bunkhouse near the lake.

She'd snuck out in her white nightie and glided like a fallen angel just to be with him. He parked his patrol car and looked around half expecting to see her, but saw Toby instead.

Blaine made his way up onto the porch with a heavy heart. Kaylee had been dealt a shitty hand in life, and it didn't seem to be getting any better.

"How's the neighborhood bitch?" Toby offered him a beer.

"You slept with her, not me."

"Trust me, you didn't miss much. Hell, I honestly don't remember it." Toby took a slow sip of his beer.

"Any movement around here?" Blaine asked.

"Haven't seen anything out of the ordinary."

"Where are the girls?" Blaine asked.

"They both mentioned something about washing their hair. I can only hope they're in the same bathroom."

Blaine thought about that for a minute.

"Damn," he muttered, lifting the beer to his lips. "That paints quite a vivid picture."

"Don't it though?"

Blaine looked out over the half-frozen lake with the moon dancing across the broken ice. "Amazing view."

"How do you feel about being a best man?"

Blaine patted his heart. "You're really serious about this, aren't you?"

"As a heart attack."

Blaine glanced at Toby. A slight glimmer flicked in his eyes. "You cryin', man?"

"Screw you, asshole."

"You shouldn't talk to your best man like that."

"Jerk," Toby muttered, tossing back his beer.

Blaine couldn't help himself, he had to laugh. The only emotion Toby had ever shown, other than when his mother had died, was anger. Toby had a short fuse and flew off the handle frequently, but over the last few months, Blaine had noticed a big change in his best friend—one for the better. "Emma is a good woman."

"Stay the hell away from her," Toby said.

"Won't be a problem." Blaine finished his beer. "I'd better get a few hours' sleep. I've got to relieve your dad at three."

"That sucks."

"Just like the rest of my life." Blaine stood and looked at his life-long friend. "Don't say a damn thing about things looking up."

Toby nodded, but didn't keep his trap shut. "Emma went over those files, and nothing jumped out at her that would put you in trouble, but—"

"I don't want to hear this."

A firm grip on Blaine's arm stopped him from entering the house. "Kaylee knows more about De Luca's illegal operations than she's let you know about."

Blaine yanked his arm away. "I told you—"

"She going to have to face a grand jury and testify against them. She's going to need your support."

"My support? Come on, man. She needs a good lawyer, and she needs to get her life back on track."

"And so do you."

"Do we have to have this conversation?"

"Yes," Toby said. "You've been lost ever since she left. And now she's back and you're still lost. Make it right."

"It's not just up to me." Blaine kicked off his boots. "Kaylee has to want to be back, and I don't think she does."

JEN TALTY

"She's afraid for her life," Toby said. "And she has good reason to be. Don't mistake her fear for trepidation about you. She still loves you. It's obvious."

It wasn't that obvious to Blaine.

246

12

K aylee tossed and turned for about an hour, but sleep eluded her. Even with a few drinks, she couldn't force her body to rest. She took a quick shower, threw on some sweats, and decided to check out her father's closet. Maybe she could find something in there that could shed some light on a man she was finding she didn't really know. The idea her father was sleeping with Rachael made her stomach turn. It wasn't just the age thing, but Rachael had been her friend.

Her nostrils were assaulted by a combination of her father's pine-scented aftershave and that rosy smell. *Rachael.* Now she knew why that smell seemed familiar. It was the same body spray Rachael wore.

Letting out a long breath, Kaylee shuffled through her father's suits and casual clothes.

She stood in the large closet with her hands on her hips and looked up at the shelves. "I've got to get those down."

"I can help." A dark, sexy drawl came from behind her.

She jumped. "Damn you, Blaine. Please stop sneaking up on me."

"I thought you might be sleeping, considering the condition I left you in." Blaine reached up and pulled down one of the boxes.

"Not enough alcohol to put me to sleep." Kaylee rubbed her temples, but she'd had enough alcohol to give her a mild headache. "Just put it on the bed and then get the rest of them down for me."

"You want to go through them all tonight?"

She climbed up on the bed and tucked her feet up under her butt. "Why not?" She shrugged.

He plopped a second box down on the floor and joined her on the bed. "I had other thoughts." His long fingers pushed back the hair that had fallen toward her face.

She glanced up at him. His eyes were dark but playful. "Let me go through this one box, okay?"

"Sure," he said.

She flipped open the box and pulled out some old pictures of her parents. "Wow, they look so young."

"There's Hadley." Blaine pointed to a group photo.

"And Mrs. Hicks?" Kaylee questioned as she took the photo from Blaine. The picture was taken on Thief Lake, and it looked as if Hadley and Linda had been a couple as Hadley's arm was looped over Mrs. Hicks' shoulder. She turned the picture over to see if there was a date. "This was taken about three months before my parents married."

"How far along was your mother when they got married?"

"I think about four months or so." Kaylee hadn't thought about her paternity since she'd left all those years ago. It bothered her father and back then, she didn't care. Today, she seemed to care. A lot. "What are you thinking?"

"We know Hadley and your mom had a thing way back when. Rumors have always been that Hadley got his heart broken. I guess I just assumed it was by your mother."

"Are you suggesting Hadley and Rachael's

mother did the wild thing?" Kaylee fumbled through a few more pictures, but whenever she came across Mrs. Hicks, she was with her husband. Life was strange.

"Hadley said Linda married Jack because she was pregnant. I've always thought it was a case of love at first sight." Blaine rubbed his jaw. "I think I need to call Hadley again."

"I was always told that the moment Reverend Hicks met his wife, they were madly in love. They up and ran off for a quickie wedding—"

"Because Linda Hicks was pregnant with Rachael?"

Kaylee dropped a picture to her lap. "Wait a minute. Then you think Hadley could be Rachael's father? Gross."

"I don't know what I think, except there was a lot of bed hopping going on with these people." Blaine dug into the box and pulled out more pictures. They spent the next hour making piles based on the year and who was in it. The only thing that jumped out at her was the possible relationship between Linda Hicks and Hadley, which really had nothing to do with her.

"My mother never looked happy. Not even

when she was pregnant. I loved being pregnant, feeling Deslin move."

"It was pretty incredible," Blaine said, fanning his hand across her middle. "You were beautiful."

Covering her hand over his, she locked gazes with him. "You used to complain when I snuggled my belly up against you. You told me you couldn't sleep, but you never pushed me away."

He closed his eyes for a moment. "I liked feeling him move, too. I'd like to go visit his grave with you."

"Before I left for Europe, I used to go there for hours, hoping I'd see you there." She'd wanted to ask for his forgiveness and start over with him. But, he never did. He never tried to call or contact her in any way, not even when she'd filed for divorce. "The divorce was the only stipulation my father had made when he'd offered to support me financially."

"I saw you at the grave a few times," he said softly. "But then you went to Europe and then the divorce papers came, and I just thought you wanted nothing to do with me anymore."

"I thought maybe it would get your attention," she admitted, stacking the photos back into the box. "Maybe you'd come fight for me."

"It got my attention all right."

"I was playing a childish game, and it backfired on me."

He shifted his stare from the box to her. "Are you trying to tell me that you filed for divorce to try to get me back?"

"Pretty stupid, huh?"

"Stupid doesn't cover it, babe," he said dryly. "My mother told me not to sign those papers. She begged me to come home for a visit, and every time she tried to bring up your name, I'd hang up on her."

"So, you signed the divorce papers and gave up."

"What would you have done in my shoes?" he asked. "You should have tried to contact me directly."

"I didn't know where you were, and no one would tell me. Your father called me all kinds of names, even Rachael gave me the cold shoulder when she'd come home from college. It was the only way I could think of to get a hold of you."

"You could have thought of something less drastic, like a simple note. I did have a lawyer who would've forwarded a message just as easily as divorce papers." He raked a hand through his hair. "I kind of took that as 'get the hell out of my life.'"

"I guess I would, too," she said as she fluffed the pillow. "I listened to all the wrong people. I believed the worst of you."

"I can't say I helped my own cause much." Blaine sat down on the bed, taking her hand in his. "I wanted you to go to the hospital the day before. You kept having those pains, and I didn't think it was normal. I just had this gut feeling something was wrong."

"The doctor told me that in the seventh month, you could have Braxton-Hicks contractions, and to just be still until the next appointment."

"But those weren't Braxton-Hicks," Blaine said softly. "I must have made you feel so bad."

"When the doctor told us that the placenta had separated from my uterus, I could see the 'I told you so,' in your eyes." Tears streamed down her cheeks.

He lifted her hand, his lips felt warm and tender against her skin. "It was a look of guilt and shame. You almost died because I'd left you alone to go hang out with my buddies." He pushed the box out of the way and pulled her into his arms. "If I hadn't left, things might have been different."

"Oh, Blaine." She cupped his face. "There wasn't anything you could've done to prevent what happened."

He looked deep into her eyes. "I'm sorry, Kaylee. I should've tried harder. I should have followed you to Europe. Hell, I should have talked to you before you left."

"We can't change the past."

"No, we can't." He took her hands in his and kissed her palms. "We can't take back what we did to each other, but we can move past it. I've missed you."

"I've missed you too," she whispered. "But I'm in some serious shit."

"I know."

"I'm going to have to go back. I realize that running away won't solve my problems."

"I'm glad you finally get that." The bed rumpled beneath her as he flipped over, placing his head in her lap.

She smiled, running her fingers through his long, dark hair. She wanted to start over with him. Begin a fresh, new life. "He knows where I am. That means he knows who is important to me. He wants me, and it won't matter who he kills in the process."

"Coming after a cop tends to piss people off."

"He might not come after you, but those you love," she said with a shaky breath. "Emma's going to help me, but I get the feeling that my days here are numbered. I've got a lot of stuff on Nino." She placed her finger on his lips. "While I'm gone, would you take care of the house for me?"

"Do you plan on coming back?"

"I don't know," she said. "I don't have any idea what will be expected of me when I turn over what I've found. I don't know if what I did will be used against me or forgotten."

He closed his eyes. "Your life will belong to the government until they're done with you. It could take months, even years."

"Blaine, open your eyes and look at me."

His eyelids fluttered open.

"For the first time in years, I feel like I could do something good with my life. Do the right thing. I have to do this."

"I know," he admitted. "And I'm proud of you."

The pounding of her pulse quickened. "Thank you," she said softly. "That means a lot to me."

"I'll take care of this place, but I won't own it. You understand?" He sat up, cupping her chin. "This is your home."

"Home? I don't know about that." Even if she could free herself from the mess she'd created in Chicago, would she come home to this house? To

Blaine? "Can we visit Deslin's grave after church tomorrow? I haven't been there since I got back."

"I'd like that," he pulled her head toward his and brushed his lips against hers.

"Wait."

"What now?" he said impatiently.

"Nothing." She wanted him; he wanted her. For this moment, that was all that mattered.

———————

Blaine could feel Kaylee give in to the moment. He had no idea if it would last, and frankly, he didn't care. Kaylee was going to have a long road ahead of her. And even with immunity, it would be a long time before Kaylee could do anything but focus on fixing her life.

Hopefully when it was all said and done, he'd be more than just a part of her past, but perhaps a part of her future.

His tongue swirled inside her mouth. She tasted like fresh cantaloupe. Smelled like a warm summer night.

Kaylee wasn't running anymore. At least not from her mistakes.

But for now, her body molded against his. She

responded to his touch with soft moans and gentle tugs at his clothes, pulling his shirt out of his jeans. She'd always been a passionate woman, even their first time together. He knew then it would never get any better than her. He'd never been able to find a woman quite like Kaylee. No one ever loved him the way she did. "You're amazing," he said as he nibbled at her stomach, lifting her shirt over her head. "So perfect, so beautiful."

"You're not so bad yourself." She smiled at him while managing to remove his shirt and then started on the button at the top of his pants. He rocked back on his heels. "Take off your bra."

She found the front clasp, opening it slowly as she rolled it off her shoulders, then held it up, dangling it in front of him.

He snagged the lacy fabric and tossed it to the floor.

"Anyone ever tell you you're a tease?" He rubbed his forefinger with his thumb in anticipation of squeezing her nipple until her eyes rolled with pure pleasure.

"Yeah," she said. "You. Every time I did this." She leaned forward, her lips so close to his, he felt her hot breath on his skin. Then she dipped her head, licking his nipple. Her hand rested on his stomach, her fingers barely caressing his skin.

He groaned as she continued to toy with him. Kissing his neck. Biting at his earlobe. Her hands all over his chest and back. She traced his lips with her tongue.

"I can think of better things to do with your tongue." He quickly cupped the back of her head and shoved his tongue into her mouth, their lips rubbing against each other so hard, they'd be swollen. He grabbed her by the thighs and lifted her up. She wrapped her legs around his body as he pushed her back onto the bed. He pried his lips from hers, only to seek out her breasts. She arched her back, guiding his lips to her soft, full mounds. His hands pulled at her sweat pants and panties, yanking them to her knees, before adjusting his body so he could pull them all the way off.

He sat between her legs as she let her knees fall to the sides, giving him a birds-eye view. Her fingers made small circles around her nipples.

"You really are a tease." He gently touched the inside of her thigh, just above her knee. "You're killing me," he said, gliding his finger up her soft skin, watching her hands dance across her breasts in slow, delicate strokes. She moaned as he inserted his fingers. She was moist, hot, and ready. He watched his fingers glide in and out of her, her head rolling from side to side. All he wanted to do was please her and not just sexually. He wanted to give her the world. She deserved it.

He raised his fingers to his mouth, tasting her, then began undoing his pants.

"No," she said, raising her head up.

"No, what?"

"You don't get to do that."

He smiled. "Don't like being teased?"

"I don't mind that you stopped." She scooted to her knees. "You don't get to take your pants off."

She reached out and cupped him.

"And...why..." he panted. "Not?"

"Because that's my job."

He cupped her face, dropping his head to her forehead. "Then what are you waiting for?"

"Lay down," she whispered, squeezing a little harder.

He wasn't about to argue with that. He crawled toward the headboard and rolled to his back. She straddled him just below his knees and started unbuttoning his pants. He put his hands behind his head and just watched as she lowered his zipper, then tugged at his pants and boxers, successfully gliding them all the way to his feet.

"Like I said." She smiled as she dropped his pants to the floor. "You're not so bad yourself."

He groaned as she cupped him with one hand, while the other rolled across the tip. "You keep teasing me like this…"

Her mouth covered him. "Christ," he whispered, reaching down, brushing her hair out of the way. There wasn't any other woman who could make him feel the way she did. Her hands and mouth moved over him in an erotic dance. He would forever be lost in her.

He lifted his upper body off the bed, cupping her face, pulling her off him. "Come here."

She kissed her way up his torso, her hand still stroking him, bringing pleasure she could only deliver. Her hands were pure magic. Their mouths met in a sloppy, but purposeful kiss. He pressed her back to the bed. "I need my wallet," he whispered as he quickly stepped from the bed, finding his jeans, his wallet, and then the condom. As he slid into the bed next to her, she took the foil from his hand, held it up in the air, and stared at it.

"He was only with us for a short time," she said. "But he was loved."

Blaine lay on his side, his hand resting on her flat stomach. If he could take away all their pain, he would. "I think of him...and you...every day."

She turned her head. "Every day?"

He nodded. "I often think about what he might look like today. I can see the three of us walking together along the side of the lake. Or going for a canoe ride."

"I often imagine what it would have been like at our house...just you and me...and Deslin...on Christmas."

"That's a sweet thought." He took the condom from her hand and tore it open, then wrapped himself in the latex. He didn't want the barrier, but they couldn't bring Deslin back. "You're a good mother."

"I wasn't a mother very long," she whispered.

"Doesn't matter. For his short time with us, he had the best mother in the world." He ran his fingers across her cheek. "I still love you, Kaylee."

"I love you too," she said. "I never stopped."

He rolled over on top of her, spreading her legs. His arms held his upper body over hers as he pushed slowly into her. "I'll always love you."

"Put your weight on me."

"I'll hurt your back."

"I don't care," she said. "I need to feel you. Hold you. Don't make me beg."

He raised his hips, then plunged into her. She arched her back, her hands digging into his shoulders, trying to pull him closer.

He went from resting on his hands, to lowering himself to his elbows, his hips thrusting gently in and out. "I don't want to ever hurt you again."

She ground against him, her breath labored. Soft moans echoed as she rolled her head side to side.

"Look at me," he said.

She ran her hands up his back, across his neck, and through his hair before she opened her eyes. "I need you."

"Keep your eyes open," he whispered, doing his best to control himself. He could easily pound himself into her over and over again until he reached his own climax, but this wasn't just about him. About his need to be with her again. She needed strength and support. She needed to know that someone was on her side and would stay there no matter what.

He could give her that, even if meant he had to let her go.

"Never forget this," he whispered, burying

himself deep inside her. "Remember I've always loved you." He kept the pace slow, and she kept her eyes focused on him, even as her body rocked with pleasure, bucking beneath him. He grunted, trying desperately not to slam himself inside her, but she wrapped her legs around him, her heels digging into his ass. He could only hope he wasn't hurting her as his own climax built around her convulsing body.

"It's okay," she whispered. "Lay on top of me like you used to. Let me hold you. Rub your back. Let me remember."

Slowly, he put his full weight on top of her, his face nuzzled in her neck.

He could feel her heartbeat, and he never wanted to let go. They shared pain. They shared love. Now he wanted to share a life. He could only hope that would be possible some day.

"You okay?" he asked.

"I'm perfect."

He lay on top of her for a short time before rolling to his side and taking in her beauty once again. "I meant everything I said."

She propped herself up on her elbow, her hand holding up her head. She'd never been shy about her body, and thankfully, she still wasn't. "I know."

She leaned in and kissed him tenderly. "I might have a world of regret. But I don't regret being with you. Ever."

"You're going to get me all hot and bothered again."

"Not hard to do," she said. "Do you hear something?"

"No," he said, but lifted his head from the pillow. "Why?"

"I thought I heard someone."

Blaine turned his head to the side. "I do hear footsteps."

"Yo, Dark Man," Toby's voice rattled as did the door.

"You open the door, and you're a dead man, " Blaine said.

"You shouldn't say shit like that to me. You know that just makes me want to open the door more."

"Just give us a couple of minutes," Blaine said, covering Kaylee's beautiful body with the sheet.

"Well, hurry up. I think I found something you two might want to see," Toby said.

"Relax." Blaine shifted to the side of the bed.

"Oh, no, you're not going to let him in here. I'm naked."

"So am I, and he already knows what we were doing."

"That is so not the point." She pulled the covers up to her chin.

Blaine let out a slight chuckle and found his pants, hiking them to his waist. "You can come in now," he called, running both hands through his hair.

"Didn't mean to interrupt," Toby said.

"What do you want?" Blaine asked.

"We found the secret room."

Blaine stuck a finger in his ear. "Come again?"

"You found the room?" Kaylee sat up, holding the covers to her chin.

"Hi, Kaylee." Toby smiled as he sat on the edge of the bed.

"If you value your life, you will move," Blaine said.

"Sorry." Toby stood up and threw his hands wide. "Geez."

"Cut the crap. Where's the room?" Kaylee said.

"Emma was going over some of those documents Kaylee gave her and decided to fire up Rutherford's computer. The first thing that came up was a web cam of the perimeter of the house."

Blaine glanced at Kaylee, her eyes wide. "This could tell us who killed him."

"If there are tapes," Toby said. "So far, all we've got is live footage."

"I lied to you, Blaine," Kaylee said.

"What? When?"

"I hid some documents in a secret compartment of the safe."

"I know," he said, rubbing his jaw. "Emma told me. But she didn't tell what the documents said. Anything else I should know?"

She shook her head, and that was good enough for him. He looked at Toby. "Mind letting us get dressed?"

"I'm not stopping you."

"Get the hell out." Blaine reached behind him, grabbed a pillow, and tossed it at Toby. "We'll meet you…"

"Rutherford's office," Toby said. He turned and closed the door behind him.

"I can't believe that room exists, and that Dad might have had this house bugged. Oh, God." Her eyes went wider as she pulled the covers tight and glanced around the room.

Blaine wanted the house to be under major surveillance. It certainly would make his job a whole lot easier, but he didn't want his or Kaylee's private moments, or anyone else's for that matter, caught on tape. "Don't worry. If there's a tape of what just happened, I'll take care of it."

"That's so embarrassing. Would you give me my clothes, please?"

Rutherford was a paranoid man, always thinking people were out to get him and his millions. He never believed that anyone did anything without motive. Blaine believed that too, but love could certainly be a powerful motive.

He found her clothes and handed them to her. "Did your father have girlfriends that you know of after your mother died? While they were married?"

She shook her head. "You'd probably know more about his life than I do, since you lived here and spoke with him."

Blaine raked his hand through his hair. "He was acting kind of weird the last few months."

"What do you mean?" She ripped back the covers, exposing her fully clothed body.

"I don't know. He was more paranoid than ever."

"Now that *is* odd," she agreed. "I want to know what happened to him and Reverend Hicks. They were like brothers. Always golfing and hunting together."

"I think Jack was having an affair with your mother."

Kaylee's beautiful face scowled. "You know Jack accused me of being just like Mom when I found out I was pregnant. Then after you and I got divorced, he had the nerve to say, 'I told you so.' For some reason, he doesn't like me much."

"I think he might be your father."

Her already porcelain skin turned paler as the color drained from her face. Her body trembled when he held her by the arms for support. He hadn't meant to spring it on her like that, but if there were tapes, she might see something totally shocking, and he wanted her to be prepared.

"I don't want him to be my father."

"There are worse things than that, Kaylee."

"I suppose." Water welled in her crystal-blue eyes. "But even if the Reverend Hicks slept with my mother, so did half the town. Honestly, I could belong to the toothless man who waters the plants in front of the general store."

13

S tanding at the entryway of her father's office, a flood of memories crashed in Kaylee's mind. She could hear the arguments he'd have with business associates on the phone. She could feel the wood floor vibrate when he paced back and forth, phone to his ear, papers in hand. He lived for his company.

But she also remembered the tender touch of his fingers brushing back her hair when he tucked her in at night. He'd tell her not to worry about her mother and that he'd take care of everything. To let him worry, and for most of Kaylee's childhood, she'd done just that. Until her mother took a turn for the worse, and Kaylee started thinking independently.

She swallowed. The room that looked exactly as she'd remembered, except for one thing. A picture of Deslin stood proudly on his desk. She stepped into the office and picked up the picture, sucking in a breath.

"I can't believe he kept that," Blaine said.

Toby and Emma stood on the other side of the desk, remaining silent.

"You gave this to him?" She glanced over her shoulder.

"Right before I left for the city. I thought he might change his mind and tell me where you were. I left the picture on the table in the front hallway, reminding him that Deslin was his grandson." Blaine's fingers pressed into her back as if he was leaning on her for support.

"I believed he…I didn't think he cared."

Blaine reached for the other picture on Rutherford's desk. "Holy shit."

"What?"

"It's our wedding picture."

"He didn't even give me away." Kaylee glanced at Blaine. "He didn't come to the wedding."

"He was a stubborn man," Blaine said.

Stubborn and foolishly proud. When Kaylee had given birth, she'd lost a lot of blood. There were times she couldn't open her eyes, but she could hear the people around her talking. She heard her father tell someone that if they ever mentioned Kaylee's paternity, he'd make sure that person paid for their betrayal. She'd also heard Blaine and her father go at it about money, among other things.

"The check," she whispered. "It just appeared in your coat?" She blinked. "Blaine, the funeral costs. The wedding. Could we have misread his intentions?" In the hospital, she'd allowed the doctors to pump her full of drugs while trying to deal with the loss of her son and her identity as Rutherford Mead's only child. She had felt lost... alone; Blaine had withdrawn from her. Then she waited for the voices to come, like they had for her mother. She waited for months, but they never came. When she finally had the strength to come back and face Blaine, he'd left town.

"I confronted him." Blaine raked his hand through his hair. "He accused me of being responsible for his grand...oh my God. He said his grandson."

"Why would he demand I divorce you in order to get his help?" Kaylee stared into Blaine's shocked eyes.

"Maybe he wanted to see what Blaine would do," Emma said softly.

"That certainly sounds like something that man would do. Always trying to test people's loyalties and screwing with their minds," Toby said.

"My father used to get a kick out of Rutherford's games at work," Blaine said. "No matter how hard Rutherford tried to rattle my dad, he just couldn't." Blaine set the pictures down. "I'm not sure Rutherford ever really officially fired anyone, he just got them to quit."

"I wish I could know for sure how he felt. Was that money supposed to help us or rip us apart?" Kaylee turned, resting her head on Blaine's shoulder.

"Doesn't really matter at this point," Toby said. "If he was trying to help, he certainly had an odd way of doing so." Toby pointed toward the small space in the back of the office.

"That's not a secret room; it's the closet where he kept his gun collection. He had to keep them under lock and key because once my mother found them and ran around the house threatening to kill everyone."

Emma lifted a brow.

"Like I said before, it wasn't so cool living here."

"I didn't know," Emma said.

"Not many people did."

"Nor did they know about the staircase behind the gun collection." Toby pointed.

"Holy crap." She leaned over Toby's shoulder. "It's dark."

"Do I have your permission to search that room?" Blaine said.

"Oh, good Lord in heaven. You realize that if I decided not to take the house, you'd own it?" She gawked at Blaine. "Or have you ever thought about just throwing the book out the window?"

He glanced at Emma. "I did that once. Now a couple of people are dead."

"Oh," Kaylee glanced between the two of them. "You have my permission."

"Thank you." Blaine squeezed her arm. "Let's get some flashlights."

"I'm not going down there." Dark, small spaces didn't do anything for Kaylee but give her the creeps.

"Yes, you are." Blaine gave her his best cop look. Damn. He was good. At everything.

"I'll see what I can find on this computer," Toby said. "Maybe there are all sorts of live cams around this place." Toby glanced up as he sat behind the desk. "I can do that, right?"

"Kaylee?" Blaine questioned. "Mind if Toby checks out the computer?"

"Sure, but isn't that stuff new technology?" Kaylee asked.

"Not really. This stuff's been around longer than you think." Toby clicked away on the computer as Emma stood behind him with her hand on his shoulder.

"Come on," Blaine coaxed.

"Can't we do this later? Don't you need some sleep or something?" Kaylee's airway constricted and her body shivered uncontrollably, but she wasn't cold.

He glanced at his watch. "I'll sleep, eventually."

The staircase wasn't much of anything but a deadly trap. A twisty ladder at best. Blaine held the flashlight in one hand and her in the other. "I see a switch."

"I hope we don't go boom," she muttered.

"Don't say shit like that to a bomb squad guy." Blaine turned to face her. "Don't move." He waved his finger at her.

As if she would dare set foot on a floor she couldn't see. She gripped the cold, small metal that was meant to serve as a railing while Blaine fumbled across the room, hitting a few things on the way and sounding off numerous curses.

A loud hum whistled in the air, the lights flickered, then flashed brightly in a small cubical of a room set up with all sorts of gadgets, televisions, and a computer.

"Hot damn," Blaine said, then started pushing buttons and more noises filled her ears.

"My mother wasn't completely crazy," she whispered, looking around the room. "No wonder I never got away with anything."

"You were always grounded." Blaine looked amused. "He had to have known about us all along if this was all hooked up. Look." He pointed to one of the screens. "That's the bunkhouse." He smiled when he glanced over his shoulder. "We had a lot of fun in there."

"Oh, God. Please tell me web cams weren't readily available back then."

"If Rutherford knew what we were doing in there, I'm sure he would have murdered me long ago."

"Doesn't make me feel any better." She rubbed her temples. "I shouldn't have assumed he was trying to buy you off."

"It wasn't like he supported us at all. Everyone thought he'd turned his back on you when we got married. As far as that check goes, only he knows what it meant." He brushed his lips against her temple. "And we can't change the past. But this all makes me wonder what kind of game your father was playing with all of us."

Blaine sat down at the desk and flipped a switch and the rest of the televisions hummed to life. Almost every room was illuminated on those screens.

She swallowed the lump in her throat. Her father had always told her to make sure she knew what was going on, even inside her own house. She'd never really understood what he meant, until now. "Why would he do all this?"

"Damn it. Toby, can you hear me?" Blaine yelled in the direction of the stairs.

"What's up?"

"Call your dad, I need him here. Now!"

"I'm on it," Toby yelled back.

"Why?" Kaylee asked, taking a step closer, peering over his shoulder to see the computer screen. "I don't understand."

"These folders are dated and contain video and still pictures." Blaine tapped the screen.

"How can you tell?"

"By the file extension. I'm going to need to confiscate all of this, but I want to see it first with Dave before I take it to the station."

"You think my father's death could be documented?"

"Could be."

"My mother's suicide could be documented, too," she said. Not something she wanted to remember, much less see.

"Let's go through the desk drawers and files." Blaine opened up the center drawer, typically used for pens and pencils and such items. "Why don't you start with that box over there?" He pointed.

"Okay," she managed, still stunned by the secret side of her father she hadn't known existed, yet everyone else suspected. Once, when she was about twelve, Rachael had spent the night and talked her into sneaking outside with a beer and a cigarette. Her father had been at a business meeting and her mother drunk and passed out on the couch. She had no idea how her father had found out that she'd had her first drink and cigarette that night. Now, she did.

She glided her hand across the top of the box. No dust. That meant her father was here often; he hated dust and dirt. 'Neat freak' didn't begin to describe his fastidiousness. Her hands trembled as she lifted the box top and peered inside.

"Books," she mumbled.

"What kind?" Blaine asked.

"Not sure." She lifted a maroon, leather-bound book. It looked like one someone would buy as a journal. The edges of the paper were silver-lined, and it felt expensive in her hands. She flipped open the book to a random page and immediately noticed her mother's sloppy handwriting. "I think it's a journal or diary."

"Whose?"

"Wow," she made out the date. "This is from the year I was born."

"Read something."

The noise he'd been making stopped, and she glanced over her shoulder. Blaine smiled warmly, giving her a knowing nod. She took a deep breath and decided to stay on the page she was on.

I felt the baby move today. I love him or her so much it hurts, but the voices say the baby is evil and will destroy everything. I try to tell the voices to leave me alone. I even tried to tell Rutherford, but he got mad because I interrupted him. I remember Great Aunt Marie used to hear voices. Mommy said she was nuts. Am I nuts, too? I hope not. I want to be a good mom to my baby, but I keep having these desires. The voices say I have to. Most of the time I like it, but later, I feel bad. Like I'm dirty. Maybe I am crazy like Great Aunt Marie.

Warm pressure came from behind her. "It's okay, babe. I'm here," Blaine whispered in her ear. "You want me to look at it?"

She shook her head. Part of her wanted to feel closer to her mother. To try to understand her. Another part wanted to make sure she wasn't anything like her mother. She flipped to another page at random.

The doctor says any day now. The voices say the baby is damned. My baby can't be evil. I don't care what the voices say. My baby will be loved and when the voices leave me alone, I can love him or her. I think it's a her. But the voices make me do things that will make her hate me. I hope my baby doesn't hate me.

. . .

Kaylee swallowed. "I had no idea she felt this way, I mean about Dad." Strong, comforting arms came around her.

"Can you read more or shall I?"

"Yo, Blaine, my pop's here," Toby shouted.

Startled, she slammed the journal closed.

"I'll haul these upstairs, and you can go through them at your leisure." Soft lips brushed her cheek. "I'm sorry, but I'm going to have to go to work for a few hours."

"I understand." She turned and slipped into his arms, resting her head against his muscled shoulder.

"Kaylee," he murmured. "You're an amazing woman, don't ever forget that."

"I don't even know who I am anymore." And that was the truth. She wasn't really the daughter of Mr. and Mrs. Rutherford Mead, or even the bastard daughter of Roberta Mead, local crazy woman. And according to her mother's voices, Kaylee was evil.

———————

By two in the morning, Blaine's vision was blurry, and he didn't think he could look at the computer screen another second. They'd found that over the years, Rutherford had installed hidden cameras that could record anything he chose. And he did on many occasions. But there was nothing dated on the day of his death.

Blaine had started with the most recent date, but nothing on the tapes indicted any foul play. Rutherford had met with men whom Blaine figured were business associates. Hadley had been to the house, but nothing seemed out of the ordinary. So they began going backward.

Blaine was worried about Kaylee. The strong, vibrant woman who'd made the decision to stand up and do the right thing was beginning to falter on a downward spiral. He'd seen her do that before.

He arched his back. For a brief time, he'd viewed the world from bloodshot eyes, not a pretty picture, and he was the last to know how pathetic his life had become. He vowed never to let anyone control his emotions again.

Then Kaylee slammed back into his life, grabbing hold of his heart and squeezing it until it drained of blood completely. He loved her. He couldn't deny it any more than he could deny his copper skin.

He clicked on a file dating back about fifteen years ago with Roberta's name on it. He'd find the answers Kaylee needed and give her some peace. His heart would have to endure her leaving, but it didn't have a choice. He didn't have a choice. She needed to turn on De Luca. It had nothing to do with Blaine.

He wouldn't even consider the possibility that she'd come back after she'd taken care of Nino and the mess he'd created. She'd realize the need to stop running and start over with a clean slate, which didn't necessarily include him.

Blaine watched, as way too many local men he knew and respected, entered Mrs. Mead's private bedroom and then left. At least Rutherford had the decency not to install a camera in her bedroom. Why had Rutherford allowed this to happen in his own home? One could only speculate.

"I know what you're thinking," Dave pushed back in the chair, clasping his hands behind his head. "But remember, Rutherford never really acknowledged her disease, and by this point, he just tolerated it."

"You grew up around here. What do you know about them when they were young?"

"Rutherford's about five years older than me. I didn't really know him, and by the time he came back from college, Sally and I had run off and gotten married."

"I wish my dad were still alive," Blaine said, realizing his error a little too late. "I mean, to ask him what he knew, working for Rutherford and all." When Blaine glanced at Dave, he expected to see an angry man, but instead he got a dose of compassion and understanding.

"Your father was a good man, the best. And I miss him, too." Dave rested his hand on Blaine's shoulder. "But he's not here and neither is Sally. These facts I can't change, no matter how much both your mother and I wish we could."

"But if you could go back and change things, you and my mother…" Blaine let his words trail off, feeling like a stupid kid. On the one hand, he wanted them both to be in love and be happy. Lord knows they both deserved it. But he missed his father.

"Wouldn't be the least bit interested in each other." Dave rubbed his jaw and then made eye contact. "Look. I love Shima with all my heart, but I'll never stop loving Sally, and Shima will never stop loving James. They will always be a part of our lives, even if I do a crazy thing like ask your mother to marry me."

Blaine had seen the writing on the wall. His mother loved deeply, and he got the impression Dave did, too. What he didn't expect to find out was that his best friend and his boss were both going to pop the question some time in the near future. "How long have you been dating my mother?"

"Oh, I don't know. About five months or so, but it wasn't really dating. We'd just meet for coffee or a movie. Hung out like old friends. Things changed pretty quickly when we realized we felt something for each other. Neither one of us does anything half-assed."

Blaine let out a chuckle, slightly amused. He liked knowing his mother wouldn't be lonely anymore. "If you don't treat her right, you'll have to answer to me."

Dave let out a hearty laugh. "This is twice in the last twenty-four hours I've sought approval from children."

Blaine smiled. "I'm not a child, but I do approve."

"You and Toby mean the world to me."

"You get sappy, and I'll kick the shit out of you." He'd always thought of Toby as a brother, and Dave as a great-uncle or second father. Now they'd be family.

Family. Blaine took a deep breath. He'd had his own family once. He could still feel Deslin jabbing his back from his mother's belly while they tried to sleep. His beautiful baby boy had weighed less than two pounds and didn't stand a chance. His tiny little veins were too small for the needles to help sustain his life.

A firm hand squeezed his arm. "Kaylee turned out to be one strong woman. She'll get through this," Dave paused, looking directly into Blaine's eyes with stubborn resolve. "And she'll surprise you, I'm sure."

"I should get out there," Blaine said, not wanting to think beyond the next day.

Dave glanced at his watch. "Did you sleep at all?"

Blaine rubbed his unshaven jaw, although he didn't have much of a five o'clock shadow. "I'll sleep later. I should get out on the roads."

"I think we need to call State in on this one."

"I couldn't agree more, but I want to look at everything before we do. Something tells me there are hidden files on this computer."

Dave rolled his neck and then glanced at his

watch. "I need to let Shima know I won't be coming home. I don't want her to worry."

"It's two in the morning; I'm sure she's asleep."

Dave arched a brow. "If I don't call, and she wakes up, I'll be in the doghouse. Not something I'm prepared for just yet."

"Whatever. You gonna pack this stuff up? Or have State come here?"

"I think I'll check things out, meet you around eight at the station, and we'll deal with State then."

"Works for me," Blaine said. He headed up the makeshift staircase with confusion in his heart.

Only the small reading lamp was on in the den. When Blaine rounded the dimly lit corner to the hallway, he realized the rest of the house had gone to sleep. *Good for them.* He took the first step upstairs. He just had to check on her and make sure she was okay.

A small light illuminated from under the master bedroom door. He hoped she'd just fallen asleep with the lights on. It had always amazed him that she could sleep with the house lit up like it was noon on a hot summer day.

He pushed back the door with a gentle tap. She lay on the bed, ankles crossed and eyes closed. A large, blue book was open across her chest. He crept quietly across the room and pulled a blanket from the chair in the corner and covered her.

"Thanks." She shifted, barely opening her eyes. "Too tired to move." She handed him the book and snuggled deep down in the bed. "Be careful," she whispered.

"Always." He pressed his lips across her forehead and inhaled her fresh strawberry scent. He wanted to crawl in bed and hug her close, but duty called. He stopped briefly at the bedroom door and turned to look at her. She peeked open one eye and smiled, and then closed it again.

His heart slammed against his rib cage. Love really sucked when your only option was to let it go.

14

Kaylee stretched, careful of her back. Surprisingly, she felt better than most mornings, and she hadn't even taken anything last night.

The room wasn't bright, but she could tell the sun was beginning to rise and bring on a new day. She adjusted herself and then grabbed the journal she'd been reading the night before. Thus far, she'd found out that her mother struggled every day with her emotions and blamed her father for it.

Her father was a hard man—unemotional and not very sensitive. His answer to everything was, "suck it up and get over it." He had no patience for incompetence and demanded perfection from everyone. She opened the blue journal and re-read the last entry.

I'm scared. My baby is sick and no one knows what's wrong. The voices are stronger than ever. They say the devil is coming to take her away. She belongs to him, not me. I don't believe them, but then they hurt me. Rutherford just doesn't care anymore. He doesn't make me take the pills. I hate the pills, even though they help with the voices. I know my baby hates me. I think I hate me, but please don't let the devil take her. I know she doesn't really belong to him. It can't be. I won't believe it. I don't care what anyone else says, my baby doesn't belong to that man.

"What man, Mom?" Kaylee tossed the book aside. Her stomach gurgled. The words written on the page were like some kind of code. One she couldn't crack. She picked the most recent journal—the one dated the year of her mother's death—and turned to the last entry. She couldn't bear to read all the depressing entries. Might as well start backward.

. . .

I'm done. I just can't take it anymore. The voices have won. I know this now because they were right. The devil actually accused me of seducing him when he was drunk and incapable of defending himself against me. Hell, he's supposed to be a good guy, he should know better. I tried to tell him the voices made me do it, but he didn't believe me then and he doesn't believe me now. I can't tell Rutherford, he'll just get mad. Kaylee won't understand; she doesn't understand the voices. I hope she never has to hear them. They talk too much. The voices are in control now. I even tried to talk to my friend, but that didn't work.

"What friend? Who are you talking about?" Kaylee sat up, rubbing her eyes. The only thing that made sense to her was that the devil and her father were one and the same, according to her mother.

I so wanted Kaylee to be Rutherford's. She could have been his. He loves her. It's me he hates. He wishes he never married me. He said the only reason he stayed was because of Kaylee. I think the voices made him feel guilty. If not Rutherford, then my friend. He comes to visit sometimes, but never stays too long. I think the voices freak him out. I told him what they say, and I heard him and Rutherford fighting about me again. Rutherford won. He always does. I know if I leave, then everything will be okay.

That's the answer.

"Oh, no, Mommy; that's not the answer." She slammed the book closed and let out an exasperated sigh. Too many questions and no real answers.

Her cell phone rang, startling her. She slipped from the bed and tiptoed across the room to the dresser. "Blaine," she whispered, seeing his number appear in the caller ID box. "Hi," she said, feeling that connectedness she'd longed for her whole life.

"Did I wake you?" His voice was kind and sent a warm shiver down her spine.

"I finished the journals," she said, climbing back into bed. She held the phone close, as if it were him. "I'm more confused now than I was before."

"Your mother was very sick, Kaylee. I'm sure what she wrote wouldn't make much sense." His soft tone calmed her tense muscles.

"That's just it. I mean, some of it makes sense, but I don't know who she's talking about."

"Give me specifics."

Kaylee closed her eyes. "She calls Daddy by name, but then references two other people as 'the devil' and 'my friend.'"

"Does she describe them?"

"Actually, the names speak for themselves. I get the impression that the devil is someone she doesn't trust."

"Her journals document this?"

"Not really. Just says she'd tried to talk to him, but he doesn't believe her."

"But no names?"

"Some of her ramblings don't make sense." She sighed. "Blaine?"

"What is it, babe?" A tenderness in his voice sent chills up her arms, the good kind. It made her feel like things might actually be okay, but she knew that things might never be.

"I think the devil is Jack Hicks."

"Why do you say that?"

She rubbed her temple. "The opposite of good is evil, and my mother constantly rambled on about how the devil lived in the church."

"Interesting point...shit."

"What?"

"Linda Hicks volunteered at the hospital for

years. I actually think she was a nurse. She could have lied about blood results to your father."

"But that doesn't make any sense. How does that affect her?"

"Maybe she's got something of her own to hide."

Kaylee glanced at the clock—six in the morning. She knew it would be hours before he'd come home. "Still planning on going to church?"

"You up for it?"

"I want to wrap up this mystery and get on with the other crap looming over my head. I need to move on, Blaine. I need to fix my life before I end up in another place I don't want to be."

"I understand."

She said goodbye and then tossed the phone on the floor and covered her eyes with her forearm, letting out a big grunt. Things might turn out all right with this mess in Chicago, but here on Thief Lake? Nope. She wasn't so sure.

———————

Blaine stumbled into the station house just minutes before eight. His eyes were dry and itchy. A dull ache had started at the base of his neck and worked its way to his forehead. His doctor had always told him stress and lack of sleep were some of the triggers for his migraines. He opened his desk drawer and grabbed some of his so-called "preventative" medicine, popped them in his mouth, and swallowed.

Kaylee had sounded okay, but her mother's diary was damn confusing. And then there was Linda Hicks. How the hell did she fit into all this?

"Why am I here?" Hadley's voice bellowed as he stomped into the office.

"I don't know, but since you're here, have a seat."

"You didn't have someone call me, wake me up, and tell me I had to get my ass down here for a meeting with you?" Hadley didn't look too pleased. He looked downright pissed off.

"Can't say that I did, but I was about to."

"Glad the gang's all here," Dave said as he strolled into Blaine's office, looking all refreshed and awake.

That frustrated the hell out of Blaine. Dave had even showered and shaved.

"What do you two clowns want now?"

"I'd like to know who Kaylee's father is for

one," Dave said as he sat down. "That list you gave us? All came after Kaylee was born."

"You asked for a list, you didn't specify a timetable," Hadley replied defensively.

"Did you sleep with Roberta around the time she could have become pregnant?" Blaine asked, hoping this was the direction his boss had planned on taking.

"We've been through all this, Blaine. I sat in your kitchen and put my heart out on your counter."

"Tell me," Dave said. "I wasn't there."

"Christ." Hadley ran a hand through his buzzed hair. "I've always liked women, too much at times. I could never only look at one, and it got me in trouble."

Blaine glanced at Dave, who just stared at Hadley, waiting for him to continue. A tense silence filled the room.

"Hadley," Blaine finally said. "Was Linda Hicks the nurse at the hospital who told you that you couldn't possibly be Kaylee's father?"

"That doesn't matter," Hadley said, but the lines on his face told Blaine how much it really mattered.

"Why would Linda Hicks care who Kaylee's father was?" Dave asked.

"She doesn't care, as long as it's not Jack." Hadley's tight expression folded into acceptance, and he slumped back against the wall. "Linda wanted the 'respectable' kind of life. One that was the complete opposite of how she'd grown up. Jack could give her that. I couldn't."

"Were you in love with Linda?" Blaine asked.

"Like I said, I like women. Couldn't turn down a pretty face." Hadley stared at the ceiling.

"That doesn't answer his question," Dave said.

"That was a long time ago, and I'm not sure I even knew what love is. Still don't." Hadley rolled his neck.

"I heard a rumor about some kind of 'arrangement' between you and Mrs. Hicks," Dave said.

"You heard correctly. We both grew up in the trailer park and were friends, until she ran off with the good-natured Jack."

"Friends? Or lovers?" Blaine asked.

"For us, they went hand in hand. It wasn't anything bad; we just understood each other. We both wanted out of our environment. She wanted a decent man, and I wanted the world."

"Kind of like, 'I'll scratch yours, if you scratch mine,'" Dave said.

Hadley nodded. "But once she married Jack, she washed her hands of me. Not that I cared. I went off to law school."

"So if she didn't want her husband to be the father of another woman's child, why not try to pin it on you?" Blaine asked, looking for any sign of discomfort from Hadley, but only getting a smug grin.

"She didn't want it to be mine either. It was bad enough Roberta had Rutherford—who, by the way, was her first choice for a husband."

"Wait." Dave stood. "That doesn't make any sense."

"Sure it does. Linda tells Rutherford he's not the father, getting back at him for choosing Roberta over her."

"Wait." Blaine scratched the back of his head. "Mrs. Hicks and Rutherford?"

"Doubtful." Hadley chuckled. "Rutherford never liked Linda much, but Linda liked his money, and she went after him."

"Okay," Dave said. "That explains why she'd try to ruin Rutherford, but I still don't get why she wouldn't pin paternity on you."

"That's why I believed her. She had more to gain if I was Kaylee's father, keeping her husband out of suspicion. Then Roberta's diagnosis came, and we just figured Kaylee could be anyone's. Rutherford didn't want to put Kaylee through that."

"I thought Rutherford kept her diagnosis to himself until later." Blaine said.

"She'd been showing signs since she was seventeen when her older brother died in a car crash. She'd go out on binges and dance topless at bars. For years, it was just me and the Hickses who knew of her illness."

Blaine glanced toward the window. The bright sun brought with it a pounding headache. "She doesn't sound like the type of woman Rutherford wanted."

"Which is why he didn't marry her until she told him she was pregnant," Hadley said. "He wanted to make sure she'd change her colors. I think she tried, but her illness was just too strong. I also think Rutherford wanted to be a father. Anything else?" Hadley pushed away from the wall.

"Not for right now," Dave said. "But don't go too far away. I might need to ask you a few more questions."

Hadley took confident steps toward the door and paused. "I'm not real close with Linda anymore. Haven't been for years, but there is something you should know." He turned and looked at Blaine. "Linda can be vindictive."

"What are you getting at?" Blaine asked.

"She's not the upstanding woman you all think she is. She'll stop at nothing to make sure her own little world stays intact." Hadley rubbed his large hand across his face. "Rutherford changed that will because Linda started to threaten him about his and Rachael's relationship. She was going to call every reporter she could think of and try to ruin him."

"By using her own daughter?" Blaine wasn't sure what to think of this new information, or the fact that Hadley was giving it so freely.

"I'm breaking client confidentially laws here." Hadley tipped his head.

"Your client is dead. Murdered actually, so just go with it," Dave said, glaring at Hadley.

For a brief second, Blaine wanted to jump up and down and slam his hand on Dave's back. He just threw the rulebook out the door, but Blaine kept his cool and only smiled on the inside.

"Rutherford and Rachael had been seeing each other. I think the old bastard really liked the young girl, but when her mother found out, she flipped out. Went after Rutherford with both barrels cocked, saying he was taking advantage, and what a dirty old man he was. Anyway, Rutherford came to me and asked me to change his will. Said something about Linda falling from grace. I didn't understand, but hey, it was his life, and Linda could be a pain in the ass," Hadley said. "I would much rather see Kaylee get everything."

"Linda not approving of her daughter's sex life doesn't make much sense as a reason for Rutherford to change his will," Dave said.

"Linda told him Jack was Kaylee's father, and Rutherford refused to believe it."

"Why?" Blaine asked. Everyone else had slept with Rutherford's wife, why not Reverend Jack Hicks?

"Denial, I guess. Jack being so religious and all. Then the way he supposedly fell head over heels in love with Linda. Jack had always been supportive of Rutherford's decisions to keep Roberta from the institutions where they'd pump her full of experimental drugs. He even took Rutherford to a psych unit to show him what kind of life she'd be living."

"The medical world has come leaps and bounds with treatments for schizophrenia," Blaine said, rolling his shoulders. He was getting more questions, not more answers.

"This was over twenty years ago."

"Wait a minute." Dave stood and held out his hand. "First, I'm pissed as hell that you've waited days to tell us all this."

Hadley nodded.

"Second, I don't get it. Why was Jack so above reproach in Rutherford's eyes?"

"Rutherford may not be religious, but he believes in a man's word."

"I find that hard to believe. He never believed in mine," Blaine said.

"You stole his baby's heart. That meant damnation in his book." Hadley stepped to the hallway and then turned back. "I'll be at home on Sunday, then at my office all week if you need me."

Blaine focused on the birds perched on the bush outside the window. The sun was shining bright, and spring was kicking in, melting the last bit of snow. "You believe him?"

"Every freaking word." Dave ran a hand across his closely buzzed head. "But when other people play God, I think God gets mad."

Blaine sat down behind his desk, rifling through the paperwork and making notes, trying to force his mind to think logically. "Linda lied to Rutherford and Hadley, but based on the time frame, any one of them could be Kaylee's father."

"We also know Roberta had a reputation for being easy, long before her diagnosis. My brother said she'd have too much to drink and offer herself to just about everyone." Dave leaned over Blaine's shoulder. "Although, they were all just kids at the time. I'm sure not everyone had the nerve to follow it up with action. Most teenage boys are all talk, no action."

Blaine laughed. "Not this teenage boy."

"Yeah, well, when I was a kid, we got married and then let our libidos run rampant."

"Obviously, not everyone from your generation were like you and Sally, and my parents."

"That's what bothers me about this. Back in the day when people had quickie weddings, usually it was shotgun. There were whispers about the Hickses, but she gave birth pretty much like it could've happened on their honeymoon."

"Are you suggesting that Rachael isn't Jack's?" Blaine glanced over his shoulder.

"Think about it. Why would she lie to Rutherford and Hadley? Unless she had her own lie to cover up, and one of them knew what that lie was."

Blaine dropped his pencil and raised his hands to his throbbing head.

"You'd better go get cleaned up for church," Dave said. "Might want to get Kaylee to trim your hair. Actually cut it and put on your uniform."

"What?" Blaine cut his hair? Never. Well, there was one thing that would get him to chop it all off. He'd made a promise if he took over as Chief of Police he'd do it, but that wasn't going to happen, not unless Dave retired… "Oh, no. You won't be retiring for years."

"I'm done." Dave smiled. "I think I might move out to the log cabin on the farm and go back to doing things I always loved."

"You love being a cop."

"I do, but I love other things, too," Dave said, turning serious. "Namely, your mother."

"I'm not cutting my hair," Blaine protested. "Or wearing a uniform. You don't wear one."

"I do when I get the rare opportunity to be on TV, or when I want to intimidate the hell out of someone, like today in church." Dave looped his arm over Blaine's shoulder.

Blaine froze and stared at the firm, fatherly

hand patting his shoulder. Oddly, he felt as if his own father was looking down on them and smiling.

Dave cocked a brow. "Come on, son."

Blaine shrugged his shoulder. "Knock it off, boss."

"Whatever you say." Dave let out a hearty laugh. "You better go; eleven o'clock mass starts in two hours."

15

K aylee pulled the comforter up and tossed the pillows onto the bed. She glanced around her father's room, and water welled in her eyes. She'd never see him again or hear his laugh. Not that he laughed all that much, but when he did, it affected everyone around him.

The smell of coffee hit her nostrils when she opened the door and started down the long hallway toward the stairs. She'd always thought it would be exciting to turn this place into a bed and breakfast. The few college courses she'd taken had been in business. She had a fascination for the hotel environment, but had never had the chance to pursue it.

"Good morning," Emma said, smiling.

"Morning." Kaylee glanced around the kitchen. She'd have to do some remodeling, but it would be easy to break the kitchen apart and have a large, separate eating area. "Where's Toby?" Kaylee poured herself a cup of coffee and mentally noted the things she'd have to change. As if she'd be able to stay here.

"Riding around the property, making sure we don't have any company."

"Oh." Kaylee looked out the window at the lake. The ice had started to melt, and a slight ripple across the water indicated a breeze. She hoped it was a spring breeze.

"Kaylee." Emma ran her fingers through her ponytail. "I spoke with Agent Thompson this morning. You need to call him."

"Now?" Kaylee asked. Her stomach jolted the coffee back up her throat. "I'm not ready."

"I went over every document you gave me and did some of my own research. Nino De Luca is one bad apple, and you have the power to stop him." Emma's stare was paralyzing, but Kaylee could see behind the cold exterior to the warm woman who existed behind it.

"How can I stop him?" Kaylee's body trembled. Instinctively, she rubbed her lower back.

"By testifying. You're an insider with paper proof. You lied about this man and need to make that right. You've also got enough here to lock him up."

"He'll kill me." Kaylee slumped down at the table. "Did you tell Thompson where I was?" Kaylee asked, hearing her own defeated voice shaking when she spoke.

"I informed him of the situation, and he's giving us until Monday night."

"That's tomorrow," Kaylee whispered. "What's going to happen to me?"

"You'll be taken into protective custody—"

Kaylee slammed her coffee down on the table. "Arrested!"

"They won't be arresting you. They don't care about what you did; they want Nino and his family. They'll protect you from him until the trial." Emma's voice was as soft as her hand pressing firmly on Kaylee's arm.

"What if he gets off? He's good at getting people off."

"I've been informed you are just the icing on the cake. All you have to do is testify."

Every mob or FBI movie Kaylee had ever seen flashed in her memory. She'd be taken to some "safe house" and wouldn't be able to see her family. She wouldn't be able to see Blaine. She'd be caged, unable to do anything but sit around and wait.

Blaine would never wait for her again.

"When De Luca is found not guilty, I'll never get to come back, will I?" Kaylee asked, realizing that no matter what happened, she'd lose Blaine once and for all. If she ran, he wouldn't follow. If Nino got off, she'd be processed into the Federal Witness Protection Program, not much better than running. "I don't have much of a choice, do I?"

"I've contacted a friend who works for the Chicago District Attorney's office. It's highly unlikely Nino will walk. He might not go away forever, but he'll be behind bars, and you'll be on your way back here." Emma locked gazes with Kaylee. For once, her pale eyes didn't hide a single emotion. "To start over in this house and with Blaine."

"I wish my life were that simple," Kaylee said.

"I think we can make it that way," Emma said.

The door rattled, and spring air filtered into the house when Blaine stepped inside.

"You look like shit," Emma said to Blaine. "I've got some things to do."

Emma disappeared through the kitchen door.

He locked gazes with Kaylee as he leaned back against the counter and ran his hands through his hair. "You okay?" he asked.

"Not really. I'm a little wigged out about Reverend Hicks possibly being my father, which makes Rachael my sister, who had an affair with my father." She took in a deep breath, sucking up the fresh air that Blaine had brought in the house.

"A new twist. It's possible Hadley is Rachael's father."

"That's crazy." Kaylee shook her head. "What about the computer stuff?" She lifted her coffee mug to her lips, savoring the freshness. She needed something real, even if it was as simple as coffee.

"One of my guys is working with the State Police, and they're going over everything. I'm hoping they might have something for me before we head to church."

"I don't want to go. I'm afraid I might fly off the handle and say something really stupid." Her hand trembled, so she placed her coffee back on the table.

Blaine's strong arms pulled her to his chest. She hadn't realized she was crying, but her body shook and her words were broken by sobs.

His chin rested on the top of her head, all the

while his hands held her close. She could hear his heart beat in a wild rhythmic pattern that was neither fast nor slow, but calming. "I think Dave and I are onto something."

"That will tell me who my biological father is? Who killed the man I called 'Dad?'" Kaylee pulled away and folded her arms across her chest. "We have until Monday, and then I have to go back to Chicago."

"I'm surprised we have that long." He held out the newspaper.

Taking the black and white print into her hands, she unfolded the paper. "Chicago Times," Kaylee read, glancing at Blaine for an explanation.

"The front page says the Grand Jury is expected to file charges against Nino and at least five others by Tuesday afternoon. I'm sure you're wanted there ASAP."

She nodded. There wasn't another choice. The only way she'd ever truly be free from her past would be to face it head on. Something she needed to do with Blaine right now. "I'm sorry."

"Don't be sorry, babe. You're doing the right thing."

She shook her head. "Am I? Or am I running again?"

"Kaylee," he said with such softness in his voice, she wanted to smack him. "One thing at a time."

She sipped her coffee. By the time she got around to dealing with her feelings for Blaine, it could be years if she took the one-thing-at-a-time route.

"Tell me about your parents' relationship with the Hickses." Blaine said, snagging a piece of crumb cake from the kitchen table.

"My father never went to church, but Jack came by the house often. He'd pray with my mother. He'd go hunting, golfing, and fishing with my father, like other men." Kaylee stared across the room and out the window. The lake glistened in the sun.

"Tell me about everyone's relationship. The way you saw it."

"I didn't really pay attention. The Hickses came to the house often and made appearances with my parents, but she was a bitch. Mrs. Hicks would always call me 'the poor child' and shake her head at my mother. Especially when Mom would be in deep with the voices." Kaylee watched the birds flutter for a spot at the bird feeder. "Do you think Mrs. Hicks knows who my father is?"

"Maybe."

"I remember after Deslin died, Reverend

looked me square in the eye and told me that the children shouldn't have to pay for the sins of their parents. He said Deslin wasn't the only child to suffer."

"What?" Blaine's eyes widened.

"I don't really understand what he meant. Between finding that damned check, finding out my father wasn't really my father, and dealing with losing you, I just kind of let that one slide. I hope some day you can forgive me."

Blaine uncrossed his legs and pushed himself from the counter, planting his hands firmly on her hips. "There is nothing to forgive, not when it comes to our son. I loved him as much as I loved... love his mother."

"Thank you," she whispered. "I loved...love his father, too."

Blaine had stopped by his apartment to get his uniform. He probably should have showered and shaved there, but he wanted to be with Kaylee. Emma had filled him in on her revelations about Kaylee's life over the last few years, and he knew he'd have to turn her over to the feds by Monday.

Technically, she was already in police custody, but he wouldn't tell her that. Not yet anyway.

He strapped his gun in place and glanced in the mirror. He never much cared for his uniform, and lucky for him, working in such a small town meant he didn't have to wear it often.

The State Troopers had pretty much started calling the shots in this case. In many ways that pissed him off, but Thief Lake wasn't a big city and didn't have the budget, means, or manpower to hold an investigation long. He knew the State boys, and they would work together. However, that didn't make Blaine feel better.

The State had pulled something off Rutherford's computer and would be discussing it with him and Dave before church. Blaine got the distinct impression that something big might be happening at church today, something that called for him in his most official capacity. He just hoped it wasn't making an arrest of Kaylee. He wasn't sure he could handle that.

"Nice," Kaylee said. "I forgot how sexy you look in that thing."

"I hate this thing." He turned and smiled at her. "I know many cops who think the uniform gives them power."

"Anything that forces you to conform to the rest of the world makes you feel trapped," she said for him.

"Not true. I respect the law and uphold it almost to the letter. I just don't look good in dark blue, kind of gets lost with the skin tone." He smiled as she approached with a mischievous grin.

"When you're in that thing, getting handcuffed sounds like fun."

The image that popped into his head was anything but appealing. Knowing the feds were on their way to make sure Kaylee testified didn't help his demeanor at all. His face must have shown where his train of thought had drifted because she stopped mid-step, and her beautiful smile faded to a frown.

"Shall we go?" she asked, turning away, but not before he saw a tear bead down her cheek.

When he placed his hands on her shoulders, she shrugged them off and then stepped toward the door. "I'm sorry," she whispered, then glanced over her shoulder. "Please make sure I get to take care of my father's ashes and visit Deslin before I have to leave."

Blaine stood frozen in time as the blonde angel padded down the hallway and out of sight. Soon she'd be gone, and in the end, he knew deep down inside she'd move past their little trip down memory lane and move on with the life she deserved.

Blaine squared his shoulders, adjusted his belt, then headed down the same hallway, but he was determined to forget about the woman and only deal with the problem at hand, which was why he had her ride with Toby and Emma.

On the ride to the church, State had contacted him letting him know they had three possible suspects—the same ones Blaine had—but had no proof. Fortunately, the State Police were able to find encrypted files that had videos of the entire Hicks family coming and going and arguing with Rutherford the day he died.

It was time to take all three of them to the station for some official questioning.

The church came into view just as Blaine rounded onto the main drag in town. The same drag where he'd first spoken to Kaylee, kissed her, and subsequently did everything he could to get her attention, including streaking.

A line had already formed outside the church, and he could see Kaylee hooking up with his mother. He waved and then pulled into a spot where two unmarked cars were. Funny, unmarked cars were very identifiable, since no one in the world would pay money to own them. Dave pulled in right behind him and looked damned spiffy in his uniform.

Blaine glanced toward his mother, who was eyeing Dave. Guess it didn't matter the age; when you had it bad, you had it bad. He allowed himself a look at Kaylee. Beautiful wasn't a strong enough word to describe the way Kaylee carried herself. Her striking blond hair was long and luscious, but never out of control. Her sensitive blue eyes always conveyed the emotion in her heart.

Momentarily, they locked gazes. His breath hitched because the way she looked at him spoke of love and forever. Her eyes were always honest, and he only saw love.

But they both had something else they had to do.

"Blaine," one of the state detectives said.

"Nice to see you again, Andy." Blaine took his hand in a firm handshake. "Tell me what you found."

"The last person in the house was Rachael. There's no audio, but the conversation appeared heated. She paced and waved her finger in Mr. Mead's face. He seemed placid, but had an eerie smile and he shook his head a lot," Andy said, pulling a file from his car. "The only thing we really have is that they were the last three people to see him, other than his daughter."

"After he'd been killed," Blaine said.

"I'd still like to question her." Andy rubbed his chin with his thumb and forefinger. "I hear the feds are looking for her."

"They found her," Blaine said, then added, "if you don't mind, I'd like to question Mrs. Hicks."

Andy eyed his partner, who Blaine recognized as Detective Garret Newburg. They seemed to pass some silent language between themselves before Andy answered. "You and Dave can question her and Rachael. We'll take the Reverend, and we do need to ask Ms. Mead a few questions." Andy had a sympathetic look. "We'll take them in after the service."

Blaine glanced across the street; half the congregation was staring at them with wide eyes. "I'm going in." Blaine glanced at Dave who nodded but didn't budge. Blaine decided to let Dave handle the State boys for now. He needed Kaylee by his side, if nothing else than to warn her about the pending questions. Andy would be tough.

Blaine took his seat between his mother and

Kaylee, placing a hand on Kaylee's knee. Sometimes life was good. Even if for only the briefest of moments.

"Isn't Dave coming?" his mother whispered.

He planted a soft kiss against her cheek. "He's taking care of business."

"You're both scaring the heck out of the entire congregation. They are all sure you're going to arrest someone," his mother said. "Neither one of you ever go anywhere in uniform."

"I hope to arrest someone." He put his arm around a stiff Kaylee and enjoyed the eyes and whispers from everyone around them. He figured no one would ever expect to see him and Kaylee near each other, much less arm in arm.

Just then Mrs. Hicks walked down the aisle, eye to eye with Blaine. He held her stare.

"Good morning, Mrs. Walker, you look lovely today," Mrs. Hicks said to Shima. "Excuse me, but Officer Walker, would you mind leaving the gun at the door?"

"I would. I'm on duty."

Mrs. Hicks looked to the front of the church, her eyes shifting uncomfortably. "Not many people in this town have ever seen you wear a uniform, especially in church, and frankly, you are making them nervous."

"Them or you?" Blaine didn't smile, just stared into Linda's eyes, reading the fear behind them. "Are you asking me to leave the church?" Blaine asked, not wavering.

"I think it would be for the best if you and Kaylee left, but I'm not *telling* you to."

"Why?" Blaine asked.

"I don't want to say this in front of your mother." Linda gave Shima a slight smile and almost looked like she gave a shit.

"Don't hold back on my account," Shima said. "Say your piece."

"Well, frankly, the community is concerned with Kaylee's status as a murder suspect." Linda closed her eyes and held up her hand. "I know we are all innocent until proven guilty, and ultimately, it is God we must stand before, but someone found out about her dealings with the mob and the attacks on her life. We are just a little nervous for our own safety."

"Shouldn't feel nervous. I'm here," Blaine said. "Chief Whitcomb and two State Troopers are right outside."

"All because of her," Linda said.

"Actually, it's because of you, your husband, and possibly your daughter, but we can get into that after church, unless you'd like to come to the station now?" Blaine flashed his smile. Out of the corner of his eye, he could see his mother's disapproving look. He shifted closer to Kaylee. His mother's pinching fingers were too close for comfort. Besides, he liked making Linda squirm, and imagined the look on her face if he tongued Kaylee right there in church. He almost laughed out loud.

Linda pursed her lips and leaned in a little closer. "You should know that the Mayor won't approve of the Assistant Chief of Police shacking up with a good-for-nothing gangster."

"That is not very Christian," Shima said.

"I imagine this congregation wouldn't want a preacher who possibly murdered his best friend because he'd slept with his best friend's wife and quite possibly could be Kaylee's father." Blaine leaned closer. "Now, either you take your place in the front pew and let your husband give these people what they came for, and I'll escort you to the police station in private. Or maybe I'll do it right now in front of the entire freaking town."

"Have it your way, but don't say I didn't warn

you." Then she turned her attention toward Kaylee. "Ask God to forgive you."

"The only thing I need to ask God for is the strength to sit through one of your husband's hypocritical sermons," Kaylee said. Blaine pulled her close when Reverend Hicks stepped into the church. Linda walked away, smiling and waving to the congregation. Blaine knew he'd rattled her. That was the point.

16

"We know you were in his house just hours before he died. We have the video to prove it." Blaine shoved his hand through his hair. They'd been badgering Rachael and Mrs. Hicks for over an hour and hadn't gotten anywhere.

"When I left, Rutherford was alive. How many times do I have to tell you that?" Linda said, tears streaming down her cheeks. "I only wanted to frighten him."

Now we're getting somewhere. Blaine scooted his chair back in front of his desk. "Why did you want to frighten him?"

"Because he was about to ruin everything." Linda swiped at her eyes. "I only waved his gun under his nose when I realized the bastard didn't give a damn about my daughter. I put it on the kitchen table and the stupid thing went off."

"What happened next?" Blaine asked, cocking his head to one side.

"He told me he was going to tell everyone his version of the truth."

"And what was that?" Blaine asked.

"I don't know because he kicked me out before we had a chance to finish the conversation." She glared at Blaine.

"Did you leave right then?"

"I didn't have much choice; the man literally shoved me out the door. Besides, some guy was in a car in the driveway waiting to see him."

"Wait, who?" Blaine blinked.

"I don't know. I don't care. I just wanted to find a way to stop him from ruining lives."

"So you went back inside and pushed him down the stairs? Then shot him?"

"No, I left." She looked at Blaine like he had two heads. "I told him I would go to the press with the story about him and my daughter and how he practically raped her when she was barely of age if he came after my husband."

"You know that's not true."

"Fine, so their relationship was mutual, but I

had some pictures of them when she was barely eighteen, and I wanted him to know if he tried to ruin my husband, I could ruin him."

"And how was he going to ruin your husband?" Blaine asked. "Or was it you he was going to ruin?"

Linda took a deep breath and let it out with a whoosh. "Jack isn't Rachael's father."

"Come again?"

"You heard me." Linda had turned the tears off.

"Who is?"

Linda laughed. "Hadley Danks."

"Interesting," Blaine said as rolled his chair back, clasping his hands behind his head. "Does Hadley know this?"

"He asked me once, but I lied to him. Rachael's always been stubborn. Since the day she was born. Things were done on her timeline. She was almost three weeks late. However, according to my wedding night, she was right on time." Linda actually smiled. "Hadley bought it hook, line, and sinker."

"Let me get this straight." Blaine shuffled some papers across his desk and then scribbled a few thoughts down. "You had an affair with Hadley before you married Jack, and Jack had an affair with Roberta. Is Jack Kaylee's father?"

"That's the million-dollar question, but the answer is most likely a big fat no."

"Why?"

"I had hoped to have more children, but I never conceived again. I had some tests done, but it wasn't me with the problem." She lifted a brow. "Jack's sterile."

"Does he know this?" Blaine asked. How did life in a small town turn into a daytime talk show?

"No."

Another bizarre twist in this tale. "Didn't he have to go to the doctor? Isn't it documented?"

"I lied to him. I worked in the doctor's office part-time. I destroyed the evidence. He thinks I had an infection and was unable to conceive again, and we were just grateful to have Rachael."

"Does he think he's Kaylee's father?"

"I'm not sure. I told him if he ever brought it up after we'd married, I would divorce him. That wouldn't look too good, so we never talked about it."

Blaine hit the intercom button. "Stacey, get someone who can sketch a profile for me."

"Got it, boss," Stacey said over the loudspeaker.

"Is Hadley Danks Kaylee's father?" Blaine asked.

"I really don't know, and honestly, I don't give a shit. Can I go?"

"Nope. I need you to tell me about the guy sitting in Rutherford's driveway. Unless you want to confess to killing him and save me some time."

"I didn't kill him," she said.

"Wait here." Blaine rose and stepped out of the office, where Dave met him in the hallway.

"A lot of weird shit going down," Dave said.

"Oh, yeah. We need to get DNA samples from Hadley, Kaylee, and Rachael. Then we need to see if Kaylee recognizes the man who Linda saw waiting for Rutherford when she left the house."

"She didn't kill him?"

"Nope, but I think she saw who did."

Kaylee paced in the hallway of the police station. Dave and a bunch of State Police occupied Blaine's office. Everything was happening too fast, and she didn't understand most of it.

Tomorrow she'd be heading back to Chicago. She felt good about testifying against Nino, and even spoke with the FBI agent this morning after church. He promised they'd make sure she was safe and no charges would be filed against her. He all but promised that Nino would never be able to hurt her again.

They couldn't promise, however, how long it would take or if it would ever end. Blaine wouldn't wait for her long, if at all. It was too much to ask even if she knew and believed he loved her. And she did believe that. But he deserved a woman who could love him now and didn't come with baggage.

She padded down the hallway toward the window next to Blaine's office. The sun was warm, and the snow had started to melt. Small patches of green grass were trying to be seen in a sea of brown from the dead of winter. Closure. If nothing else, she'd get closure on this part of her life. She'd get to sprinkle her father's ashes over the lake, with Blaine at her side. She might even ask Toby and Emma to join them. She felt like she was at home with them.

Then she and Blaine could go visit their son, together. Grieve for him together, like they should have done years ago.

The house. What would she do with the house? She loved that house, in spite of some bad childhood memories, and wanted to make it a bed and breakfast. She wondered if Blaine would even consider living there until she could return, like she'd asked. Hoping that he would take care of it for her.

She felt guilty asking him, like it was a way to tie him to her forever.

"What are you deep in thought over?" Blaine whispered.

She jumped, dropping her purse. "Your ability to sneak up on me is making me crazy."

He bent over, picked up her purse, and handed it to her. "Everyone is willing to take the DNA tests, and I'm sure I can pull a few strings to put a rush on it." He stood next to her, gazing out the window.

"Nino sent someone to kill my father, didn't he?"

"Sit down." Blaine motioned toward the chair.

"I think I'd rather stand." The grave look on his face sent her stomach on a roll.

"Mrs. Hicks has been very diligent regarding making this sketch." He tapped the pad of paper he held in his hands.

"You expect me to recognize him?"

"I'm hoping." He ran his fingers through her hair. "Are you ready?"

She nodded and followed him into his office.

Linda glanced her way and then let her gaze fall to her lap. "I hope this helps," she said softly.

Blaine opened the pad, showing the sketch.

"Oh…my…God." She leaned back against Blaine's firm frame. "That's the guy."

"What guy?" Dave asked.

She closed her eyes, letting out a long breath. "The man who stabbed me," she said before opening her eyes again. "He goes by the name of Hector Marange. I've never actually seen him with Nino, but I've heard Nino talk about him, and I know he's the one who attacked me."

"He's in custody," one of the State Troopers in Blaine's office said. "The FBI picked him up last night on three counts of murder. I guess we can add attempted murder to the long list of charges."

"I need to sit down." Kaylee gripped Blaine's arm.

Linda gave up her seat and then followed the State Troopers out into the hallway.

Kaylee heard muffled voices, but she couldn't focus on the words. Her father was dead because of her. "Is this over?" she asked once the office had been cleared.

"Pretty much." Blaine knelt beside her. "I have some things I have to do. Will you be okay here for a few minutes?"

She nodded, unable to form words or feel

anything but numbness. She waited for Blaine to leave before she dropped her head into her hands and cried. So many mistakes. Too many lies. Her father had died because of those lies.

"How are you doing?" Hadley asked as he walked into the office with two cups of coffee. "Blaine thought you might want this." He handed her a cup.

"I've seen better days." The black liquid mirrored her feelings, dark and dismal. "Thank you." She blew into the mug. "Blaine told me you'd give a DNA sample."

She heard him take a deep breath and let it out in a huff. "I'll be honest. I'm scared."

She turned to look at him. True admiration filtered from his pale-blue eyes. He looked like the kind of man that even if he'd never found his one true love, he loved many people, on many levels. "You're not a bad guy, Hadley."

"Maybe not, but look what I've created by my selfishness." He took a seat across from Blaine's desk.

Kaylee sipped her coffee, glancing at Hadley. "It wasn't your selfishness, but other people's cruelty."

"I'm not so sure about that." He ran his long

fingers across his chin. "Looking back, I should've seen it all."

Long moments of silence followed as the minutes ticked by. She stared out at the parking lot, watching people come and go, including Rachael.

"Rachael's here," Kaylee said.

Hadley sat up straighter, and they both eyed the door as if it had all the answers.

Rachael glanced between Kaylee and Hadley then looked down at the floor. "Please don't hate me," Rachael whispered.

"Hate you for what? Sleeping with my father?" Kaylee looked at Rachael, who was dressed in a pair of designer slacks and a warm sweater. She had perfect hair to complement the clothing. The woman looked like she belonged in Stepford, except for one thing—she had real emotions behind her eyes.

"Your fath…Rutherford and I had a relationship. At first I wanted to use him, to get back at everyone. You know, shock value, but over the years, I started to care for him."

"Did he care about you?" Kaylee asked

"I think he did, but he wouldn't marry me. He made that perfectly clear. Said he'd never marry again, and I wanted that more than anything. To have a family. Children. Everything." Rachael sat down next to Kaylee. "I never meant to hurt you."

"You haven't hurt me," Kaylee took her hand.

"Yes, I did. I hurt both of you." She glanced toward Hadley. "I knew my father couldn't have kids."

"How?" Kaylee asked.

"When your son died," Rachael said. "My mother thought for sure everything was going to come out. She got drunk one night and rambled about this and that. I didn't understand most of it, but she made it very clear that my father wasn't my father. Even told me who my real father was."

"You knew we could be sisters?" Kaylee's voice rose up.

"I suspected," Rachael said. "Based on everything my mother said that night."

"Why didn't you say anything?" Kaylee asked.

"You left," Rachael said.

"I can understand that," Kaylee said.

"Also," Rachael looked toward Hadley. "I wasn't sure you'd want me as a daughter, and frankly, I didn't want to deal with it. The rumors, the gossip. What it would do to my family. I saw what Kaylee's mother's disease did to hers. Everything got so screwed up."

"You spoke to Daddy the night he died. It looked like you'd argued. Why?" Kaylee asked.

"He confided in me that you were coming home, and he was going to tell you what he'd found out."

"He knew?" Hadley asked. "And he didn't tell me?"

"He wanted to talk with me and Kaylee first, then you."

Hadley shook his head. "Then destroy your parents."

Rachael wiped the tears falling down her cheeks. "He loved Roberta, really, he did. He blamed my father for keeping her sick all those years."

"Your father says she got him drunk and seduced him, tempted him like the devil," Blaine said, leaning against the doorjamb. "I'm sorry, Rachael, but your father has some real issues."

"Don't be sorry. I've made my share of mistakes in all of this. I hope some day we can all move past this and be friends."

"After we get the DNA samples, Rachael and Hadley, you're free to leave, but don't go too far, in case I need to talk to you some more," Dave said.

"I'm always here for you." Rachael rose,

bending to give Kaylee a kiss on the cheek. "Day or night."

"Ditto." Kaylee smiled when Rachael's eyes twinkled like when they were kids. "More than friends."

"Soul sisters," Rachael whispered and turned toward Hadley. "As for you, don't expect me to call you 'Daddy,' but I'd like to have dinner with you sometime."

"I'd like that." Hadley sniffled. "How about we start with a cup of coffee?"

"No time like the present."

Kaylee listened to their footsteps fade in the distance, and then rolled her neck at the tender touch of Blaine's fingers.

"Toby will take you home. I've got some loose ends to tie up."

"Okay." She sighed. "Thanks."

"You're welcome. I'll see you tonight."

She closed her eyes and waited until she knew he was gone before letting herself take a breath. One more night. She'd cherish it for the rest of her life.

Blaine drove up Route Eight heading down the lake toward the Mead mansion on the hill. So much had happened and in just a few short days. He felt like he could sleep for a week, but that would have to wait, although he would enjoy his last night with Kaylee.

Loving Kaylee had always been easy for him. Keeping her was a whole other story, and he was about to say goodbye. At least this time he'd have the chance, even if it was as small as a bit of closure on their past.

Toby's old Jeep was in the Mead mansion driveway.

The back door opened, and Kaylee stepped out onto the porch. She held one of the posts and leaned her face against the wood. Her mouth formed a slight smile as he took a few small steps toward her.

Her hair was pulled back in a loose ponytail at the nape of her neck. She wore a pair of faded jeans that hugged her body, and one of his old shirts. She couldn't look more beautiful if she were decked out to the nines.

When he stood at the bottom of the steps, he could smell her strawberry shampoo and her vanilla lotion. Those two smells were intoxicating. He climbed the stairs and pulled her into his arms. "Hi, babe," he whispered in her ear.

She raised her shoulder, batting his lips from her ear. "What's going to happen to Linda?"

"Most likely she'll face a short jail term followed by community service for obstruction of justice."

"What about Jack?"

"Technically, he didn't do anything wrong." He stared into her beautiful, blue eyes and searched, looking for any hint of what could be.

"I spoke with Agent Thompson again. He'll meet us here tomorrow at four."

"When do you want to take care of your father's ashes and visit Deslin?"

"I've asked Hadley to come with us when I put Dad's ashes in the lake." She dropped her head to his chest. "Rutherford will always be my dad, but if Hadley really is my biological father, I want him to be a part of my life."

"He's always been a part of your life. So has Rachael."

He felt her chest rise high, and a slow sigh followed. "I suppose we've always had a bizarre connection. I just hope she can accept Hadley."

"What about me?" he asked.

She squeezed him tight and then lifted her

head. Her eyes glistened with tears. "I can't expect you to wait for me, but I want to come back here. Start a new life here."

He fanned his thumb across her tear-stricken face. He was humbled by her resolve and determination to do the right thing and start her life over.

"I love you," she whispered.

"I love you too."

"Will you watch over my house?" she asked.

"Yes," he said, not knowing what else to say.

"I've jotted down some ideas for remodeling so I can turn it into a bed and breakfast. Would you be interested in doing some of the work?"

"I'd love to."

"You could live here, if you wanted to."

He'd like nothing more, as long as it meant she'd be living here with him. "That would make it easier for me to do what you want."

"I'm sorry, Blaine, so sorry." She buried her face in his chest, and her body rocked up and down.

"Shhh, babe, don't cry." He lifted her into his arms and kicked open the door.

"Take me upstairs and make love to me. Please, Blaine."

"That was the plan." He planted a tender kiss

on her forehead. "We'll take care of everything else tomorrow. Tonight is for us."

She cupped his face and looked deep into his eyes. "Just us. No talk of the past and no promises for the future. Just right now."

Tears fought to break free from behind his eyes, but he kept them from forming. He'd have time to cry when she was gone. He needed to cherish the moment. To cherish the woman he loved.

17

S *ix moths later...*
        "Damn it," Blaine stared into the mirror as he tried to tie the bow tie to his tux once again.

"Here, let me." Toby laughed, yanking the tie from Blaine's hands.

"Isn't that my line?"

"You're freaking useless as a best man," Toby said, then got the tie done on the first try.

"I threw you a great party." Blaine scowled at himself in the mirror. He raked his hand across his hair. It was still long, but not long enough. "I can't believe I let your father talk me into cutting off some of my hair." Dave hadn't officially handed in his resignation, yet.

"According to him, you didn't cut off enough."

"Got that right," Dave said when he entered the room. "Christ, Toby. The least you could have done was shave. It's your wedding."

"It's Emma's wedding," Toby said. "All I was told was to show up. In a tux. She never said anything about shaving."

"You always going to do what your *wife* tells you?" Blaine put on his best smile. Last month his mother and Dave had eloped, and now Toby and Emma were actually having a church wedding. He was happy for both couples, but his heart ached. He hadn't seen Kaylee for six months. He'd talked to her on the phone, but the FBI kept her whereabouts a huge secret for her own protection. He had hoped, since he was a cop, they would bend the rules. But that didn't happen. They said they had bent them enough already.

Now that the trial was essentially over, and Nino and his goons had been sentenced and would be spending the rest of their days in prison, he thought Kaylee could come home. But the feds wanted to keep her in the safe house for a little while longer while they made sure all the paperwork was in order and no threats were being made on her life.

"Buck up, buddy. Just got word your date arrived." Toby slapped him on the back.

"Great. The maid of honor who didn't even show up for the rehearsal. Who is this chick anyway?"

"Emma says she's her best friend." Toby shrugged.

"I hear she's hot, too," Dave teased.

"You're a married man," Blaine said.

"I don't need a reminder on that fact. You two better get out there. Time to get this wedding on a roll before the drugs wear off of Toby."

"Ha, ha, Dad."

Blaine pushed back the door that went from a small room known as the groom-holding tank into the church. Jack Hicks had retired from the church and moved away. The young Reverend Bruster had taken over two months ago.

Blaine glanced at the preacher, who still had teenaged pimples across his forehead, and all of a sudden, he felt old. He stood next to Toby at the altar and focused on the back of the church where Dave escorted his mother down the aisle, grateful his new stepbrother had accepted his mother. Not that he'd had any doubts.

Emma's mom came next, and then a bunch of bridesmaids he didn't know too well.

Toby elbowed him. "Here comes your date."

"Great," Blaine muttered.

"Wow, check her out," Toby said.

"You're getting married," Blaine whispered, keeping his eyes to the ground, royally annoyed that everyone seemed to be pawning him off on a stranger.

"Come on, just look."

Well, he'd have to look at some point. He rolled his neck, turned his head, and choked on his own breath as Kaylee walked down the aisle in a pink, strapless satin dress, her blonde hair flowing across her shoulders.

A hearty slap on the back helped ease his coughing fit. "Told you she was a looker."

Kaylee smiled. A single tear rolled down her cheek. She did nothing to stop the tear, but no more followed. She kept her eyes locked with his as she took her place across the aisle.

In the background, the music changed, and Blaine barely noticed Emma had begun her waltz. All he could see was his angel. He wanted to scoop her up in his arms and run her home, lock her in the bedroom, and never let her go.

"My present to you," Emma whispered before she took her place next to Toby.

"I didn't get you anything," he said. His gaze

followed Emma for about a second, then he moved his eyes back to Kaylee, who stared back, smiling. "Do we have to stay? You've got enough people here. You don't need us."

"You leave, I will hurt you," Toby said. "Do you mind if I get married now?"

"Whatever," Blaine said. The next twenty minutes were worse than the last six months.

Things were happening around him. He heard voices and music, but he saw only the woman of his dreams.

"Yo, Dark Man. The ring." Toby snapped his fingers in Blaine's face.

Laughter erupted in the congregation.

"Sorry." Blaine dug into his pocket and handed Toby the ring. "I'm a little pre-occupied."

"Useless," Toby said. "Freaking useless."

Blaine smiled. "Can you finish this up? I've got some business to take care of."

Toby just shook his head and turned his attention to Emma. Blaine forced himself to watch the rest of the ceremony as his best friend said his 'I do' and kissed his bride. Toby and Emma turned as the young preacher announced them man and wife.

As Toby and Emma glided past him with smiles plastered across their faces, it hit Blaine. He'd be the one escorting Kaylee down the aisle. His brow broke out in a cold sweat, and his heart damn near pounded out of his chest.

He'd get to touch her.

"Hi," she whispered.

"Hi," he said, giving her his arm. He forced his focus down the aisle and away from everyone in the pews.

"Surprised?" she asked.

"Not the right adjective." He followed Toby and Emma around to another room where they'd have to wait for the church to empty before they'd have to go back in for pictures. Cruel and unusual punishment took on a whole new meaning. "When did you get here?" he asked Kaylee.

"Last night."

Blaine glanced at Emma and Toby, who just shrugged and went back to their own little world. "Did you know when you called the other day?"

She nodded. "Are you mad?"

"Are you here to stay?"

"Okay, time for pictures!" Emma's mother came in and started dictating this and that.

"Do we have to?" he whispered in Kaylee's ear, then pressed his lips against her skin.

"Yes." Kaylee kissed him, then left to go stand

next to Emma while a photographer snapped a million pictures.

He did his part. Smiled when he was told. But his mood was growing dark. He needed to be alone with Kaylee.

"Are we done?" he asked Toby.

"There's a second limo in the parking lot, and you've got two hours before the reception starts," Emma said.

"Just don't be late for the reception." Toby waved his finger at Blaine. "I don't want to have to hurt you."

Blaine glanced from the happy couple to Kaylee, who was backing up toward the door with a major mischievous grin across her face.

"I'll deal with you two later." He sauntered toward Kaylee.

He followed her out to the parking lot and into the waiting limo. "I'm glad you could come," Blaine said, closing the limo door and wrapping his arms around Kaylee.

"So am I." She smiled. "I wanted to surprise you."

"You did." He kissed her temple. "I followed the trial; I'm very proud of you."

"Thanks. There were times I wanted to climb

through a bathroom window and run."

"I can understand that."

"But if I ran, I would've never been able to come home."

His heart skipped at hearing the word "home" come from her lips. "Is this your home?"

She nodded. "They let me take a couple of computer classes in hotel management online under another name while I was waiting around. I really think I can turn my family home into a great bed and breakfast."

Her smile was contagious. He felt the corners of his mouth turn upward. "I'm sure you can."

She tilted her head. "You're so quiet. Aren't you glad to see me, Blaine?"

"I'm very happy to see you." He brushed his lips against hers. "Do you want me in your life? Forever?"

"What?" Her mouth opened wide. "Are you crazy? Why the hell do you think I went to all this trouble to surprise you?"

"I have no idea."

"You're teasing me."

"Not really," he whispered, pulling her to his lap.

"I love you." She nuzzled her face in his neck.

"Tell me that again."

"I love you."

"I think you might have to show me how much you love me before I fully believe it."

"That can be arranged," she said, just before her lips landed with his in a spark that ignited their passion.

The limo jerked to a stop, and he cupped her face, prying their mouths apart. "We're at the house. Close your eyes."

"Why?" She asked, covering her eyes with one hand while he guided her with the other.

"I have a surprise for you."

"Oh, I love surprises!" She giggled. "But hurry, we only have about an hour before we have to head back, and I want you naked."

He chuckled. "Naked is good." He kicked open the back door. The kitchen was still in pretty bad shape, but the new cabinets had arrived, and he had a piece of the granite countertop he picked out. "Okay, open your eyes."

"Oh, Blaine," she whispered. "You believed!"

"I never doubted," he said. "Do you like it so far?"

She cupped his face. "It's a mess, but I know when you're done, we're going to love it."

He kissed her nose. "I have one more thing for you." He tugged at her hand and then guided her up the stairs and to the master bedroom. It had been weird at first to sleep in this house without Kaylee. But after his mother put her house on the market so she and Dave could start fresh in a new home that was just theirs, he realized he was going to need to get used to a lot of new and different things.

"Our bed," she whispered.

He smiled. "It is our bed."

She turned around. "Unzip me."

"Wait."

"For God's sake, why?"

"Just give me a minute." He turned and opened the dresser drawer to the nightstand with a trembling hand. He fumbled as he pushed aside the junk until he found the box. "I don't know why I saved this, but I did." He held out the box and then dropped to one knee. "Our love never died, it just needed to be rekindled. I love you, Kaylee Mead, and I want to marry you."

"Legally, my name is Kaylee Walker."

"Okay."

"Ask me using the right name."

He shook his head. "Kaylee Walker, will you marry me, again?"

"I'll marry you." She dropped down on her knees and held out her hand. "I can't believe you kept my ring."

He slipped the ring on her finger. It fit perfectly. "I can get you a bigger one if you want."

She shook her head vigorously. "No way. I want this one."

"I love you." He cupped her chin. "I don't want a big wedding. We did that once; can we elope?" Blaine asked as he slipped the zipper to her dress down, feeling her soft skin against his hands.

"How about next weekend?"

He scowled. "Got the night shift. It will have to be the following weekend. Crap."

"What?" She fumbled with his tie and pushed his coat back over his shoulders.

"I don't have any condoms."

She laughed.

"I don't see the humor in this."

"I don't want condoms. I want you…and babies. We're getting married in two weeks. I'm not getting any younger."

"Then let's get naked."

"So romantic."

"I have my moments." He let her dress fall around her knees.

He pulled her body close against his. "I never stopped loving you." Gliding his fingers across her cheek, he added, "You are the air that I breathe."

"You are the water I drink," she said. "Forever and always you will belong to me."

He smiled. "I think that's my line."

"Not anymore." She laughed, molding her lips against his.

At that moment, Blaine knew the fire in his heart would always burn.

Thank you for taking the time to read *Rekindled!* I hope you enjoyed! Please feel free to leave an honest review. Next up in the Men of Thief Lake series is:

Destiny's Dream

Please check out my new series co-written with NY Times Bestseller Elle James! The first book is: **Secrets in Calusa Cove**

Grab a glass of vino, kick back, relax, and let the romance roll in...

Sign up for my *Newsletter (https://dl.bookfunnel.com/ 82gm8b9k4y)* where I often give away free books before publication.

Join my private Facebook group (https://www.facebook. com/groups/191706547909047/) where I post exclusive excerpts and discuss all things murder and love!

ABOUT THE AUTHOR

Jen Talty is the *USA Today* Bestselling Author of Contemporary Romance, Romantic Suspense, and Paranormal Romance. In the fall of 2020, her short story was selected and featured in a 1001 Dark Nights Anthology.

Regardless of the genre, her goal is to take you on a ride that will leave you floating under the sun with warmth in your heart. She writes stories about broken heroes and heroines who aren't necessarily looking for romance, but in the end, they find the kind of love books are written about :).

She first started writing while carting her kids to one hockey rink after the other, averaging 170 games per year between 3 kids in 2 countries and 5 states. Her first book, IN TWO WEEKS was originally published in 2007. In 2010 she helped form a publishing company (Cool Gus Publishing) with *NY Times* Bestselling Author Bob Mayer where she ran the technical side of the business through 2016.

Jen is currently enjoying the next phase of her life…the empty nester! She and her husband reside in Jupiter, Florida.

Grab a glass of vino, kick back, relax, and let the romance roll in…

Sign up for my Newsletter (https://dl.bookfunnel.com/ 82gm8b9k4y) where I often give away free books before publication.

Join my private Facebook group (https://www.facebook. com/groups/191706547909047/) where I post exclusive excerpts and discuss all things murder and love!

Never miss a new release. Follow me on Amazon:amazon.com/author/jentalty

And on Bookbub: bookbub.com/authors/jen-talty

ALSO BY JEN TALTY

Brand New Series Co-Written With Elle James!

Welcome to...Everglades Overwatch!

Secrets in Calusa Cove

Safe Harbor Series

Mine To Keep

Mine To Save

Mine To Protect

Mine to Hold

Mine to Love

Check out LOVE IN THE ADIRONDACKS!

Shattered Dreams

An Inconvenient Flame

The Wedding Driver

Clear Blue Sky

Blue Moon

Before the Storm

NY STATE TROOPER SERIES (also set in the Adirondacks!)

In Two Weeks

Dark Water

Deadly Secrets

Murder in Paradise Bay

To Protect His own

Deadly Seduction

When A Stranger Calls

His Deadly Past

The Corkscrew Killer

First Responders: A spin-off from the NY State Troopers series

Playing With Fire

Private Conversation

The Right Groom

After The Fire

Caught In The Flames

Chasing The Fire

Legacy Series

Dark Legacy

Legacy of Lies

The Buried Secret

Its In His Kiss

Lips Of An Angel

Kisses Sweeter than Wine

A Little Bit Whiskey

It's all in the Whiskey

Johnnie Walker

Georgia Moon

Jack Daniels

Jim Beam

Whiskey Sour

Whiskey Cobbler

Whiskey Smash

Irish Whiskey

The Monroes

Color Me Yours

Color Me Smart

Color Me Free

Color Me Lucky

Color Me Ice

Color Me Home

A Christmas Miracle

Spinning Wheels

Holiday's Vacation

The Brotherhood Protectors

Out of the Wild

Rough Justice

Rough Around The Edges

Rough Ride

Rough Edge

Rough Beauty

The Brotherhood Protectors

The Saving Series

Saving Love

Saving Magnolia

Saving Leather

Hot Hunks

Cove's Blind Date Blows Up

My Everyday Hero – Ledger

Tempting Tavor

Malachi's Mystic Assignment

Needing Neor